TWO A DAY

LAUREN BLAKELY

Lauren Blakely Books
powered by dogs

COPYRIGHT

ALSO BY LAUREN BLAKELY

Big Rock Series

Big Rock

Mister O

Well Hung

Full Package

Joy Ride

Hard Wood

Happy Endings Series

Come Again

Shut Up and Kiss Me

Kismet

My Single-Versary

Ballers And Babes

Most Valuable Playboy

Most Likely to Score

A Wild Card Kiss

Two A Day

Plays Well With Others

Rules of Love Series

One Night Only

One Exquisite Touch

My One-Week Husband

MM Standalone Novels

A Guy Walks Into My Bar

One Time Only

The Bromance Zone

The Best Men (Co-written with Sarina Bowen)

The Heartbreakers Series

Once Upon a Real Good Time

Once Upon a Sure Thing

Once Upon a Wild Fling

Boyfriend Material

Asking For a Friend

Sex and Other Shiny Objects

One Night Stand-In

Lucky In Love Series

Best Laid Plans

The Feel Good Factor

Nobody Does It Better

Unzipped

Always Satisfied Series

Satisfaction Guaranteed

Instant Gratification

Overnight Service

Never Have I Ever

PS It's Always Been You

Special Delivery

The Sexy Suit Series

Lucky Suit

Birthday Suit

From Paris With Love

Wanderlust

Part-Time Lover

One Love Series

The Sexy One

The Only One

The Hot One

The Knocked Up Plan

Come As You Are

Standalones

Stud Finder

The V Card

The Real Deal

Unbreak My Heart

The Break-Up Album

The Caught Up in Love Series

The Pretending Plot

The Dating Proposal

The Second Chance Plan

The Private Rehearsal

Seductive Nights Series

Night After Night

After This Niqht

One More Night

A Wildly Seductive Night

ABOUT TWO A DAY

Look, I had a rough week at work. So I escape to the beach, where I wind up rescuing the city's hot new quarterback from a rogue paddleboard, and then he rescues me that night from a s-e-x drought.

Hello O-Town. Nice to see you!

The charmer with the magic hands wants another date too, and I say yes so fast.

But the thing is I'm the team lawyer for The Mercenaries. And the morning after the sexiest night of my life, I find out the guy I plan to see again was just traded to our team.

Dating the brand spanking new star quarterback?

Off limits.

Especially when my boss blindsides me with this twist – I'm in charge of managing his reputation.

I really shouldn't invite him over late tonight then.

Truly, I shouldn't...

Contents include: sex hacks, text snafus, bedroom dares, major league dirty talking, and twists you won't see coming in this sexy sports romance.

AUTHOR'S NOTE

Dear Reader:

Once upon a time I wrote a football novella called Out of Bounds. When I bought the rights back to that novella from the publisher, I thought I would expand it into a novel. Instead, I started from scratch and wrote an entirely new football romance. But I did keep the hero's name, the heroine's profession and the setting of Los Angeles. I also kept the settings for a few scenes, such as the beach where they meet, and a movie theater where they bump into each other. But all the dialogue, interactions and emotions are brand new! In short, this is a 98% brand new novel!!! Enjoy!

Xoxo
   Lauren

TWO A DAY

A DATING GAMES NOVEL

By Lauren Blakely

Want to be the first to learn of sales, new releases, preorders and special freebies? Sign up for my VIP mailing list here! You'll also get free books from bestselling authors in a selection curated just for you!

PRO TIP: Add lauren@laurenblakely.com to your contacts before signing up to make sure the emails go to your inbox!

Did you know this book is also available in audio and paperback on all major retailers? Go to my website for links!

PROLOGUE

Drew

I've learned a thing or two from playing football most of my life. To be competitive, you need good hands and a fast mind. But nothing else matters if you don't have great teamwork.

Football's a little like good sex. No shade against solo sessions, but sex is best when you and your partner play well together. My best skill between the sheets? *Listening* to a woman in bed. I follow her cues, learn her likes, take care of all her needs.

I bring those talents to dating too.

And, fine, I'll admit that as a quarterback I definitely have an advantage in the dating department—it's literally my job to find chances and then to go for it.

So when I meet a beautifully brainy woman right before the season starts, I'm all in, making a helluva big play for her.

But then, out of nowhere, the universe sacks me.

Oof.

1

THE HOTTIE GOES KERSPLAT

Brooke

Are you kidding me?

I stare at the email from my ex in disbelief.

This has got to be a prank. Or he's doing it for upvotes on some Reddit post—*Wildest things an ex has ever said,* or something.

Or maybe I just haven't had enough coffee.

The Los Angeles sun streams through my kitchen window as I cross the kitchen to pour another cup of ambrosia. I swallow a hearty gulp and let it work its magic on my brain cells.

There.

I'm fueled up after the worst week ever and ready to read this bizarre request again.

. . .

Hey, Brookey Babes!

So, you probably follow me online. If you don't, you totally should. Started a new profile. I call it The Shirtless Esquire. You know, since I used to be a lawyer, and "esquire" just sounds so fucking cool.

Anyway, I'm doing a hot new series called "Conversation with my Ex" for The Shirtless Esquire OnlyFans page. Get this—I'll be interviewing my exes about what went wrong. It's gonna be insightful and healing, and it'll give me a chance to tell both sides of the story. And I know it's been a hot minute since we were a thing, when I think of exes, you're one of my faves. How about it? Wanna help me break the Internet?

Love ya much and always,

Sailor

P.S.: Yeah, I'll be shirtless for the convo. Feel free to do the same, but no pressure. Totally up to you.

And...I did read it right the first time.

Exasperated, I contemplate a reply. Something like: "Shockingly, Sailor, I do not want to be part of your interview series. Or to speak to you shirtless. We split because you went pants-less with other people. Maybe you should try keeping your clothes on for a change?"

Ugh.

I'd ignore the email and forget about it, but I know Sailor will call too.

And yup. My phone trills and his face flashes on the screen.

I grit my teeth, send the call to voicemail, then text a reply.

Brooke: Thanks for thinking of me. But feel free to lose my number.

Then, I block his. I down the rest of my coffee, blow out an exhausted breath, and stare at the kitchen counter, littered with reminders of my hellish week. My bottle of migraine meds got a workout these last seven days. So did my wallet, thanks to the bill from the tire shop after I drove over a nail in the grocery store parking lot *after* I got rear-ended by a mom texting in her minivan. And over in the corner, a wilted bouquet of peonies dies miserably, fallen petals collecting around the vase in a stinky mess.

Who sends flowers to someone who didn't get a promotion? My boss. Why can't Stephen make it easier to be mad at him? But I guess I should be grateful. Flowers and no promotion are still better than redundancy and no job. It's hard to get ahead in my industry, and I need the money, so I'll just have to water the peonies, smile, and go to work tomorrow, ready to do it all again.

But there's only one thing for me to do today as the weekend draws to a close.

Hit the beach and read a book.

Nothing cures a bad week like some sun and an escape into make-believe.

* * *

After a few hours spent basking on the beach, immersed in the latest escapades of Axel Huxley's vigilante-for-hire, I've nearly forgotten my ex's ridiculous request. The sea and stories have always settled me, ever since I was young. Today, the combo does its trick, washing away my week.

Normally, I wouldn't let an ex bug me so much, but I can't escape The Shirtless Esquire. He's become a *thing* on social media. My co-workers update me about his online antics, more than one of them noting how hot Sailor is.

I wish I could *whatever* him away with a pure give-no-fucks attitude, but hearing from him reminds me that in the year since we split, my dating life has been a desert.

My social calendar is the Sahara.

That's Los Angeles—a good guy who doesn't mansplain is as rare as a clear lane during rush hour on the freeway.

I set down my paperback on my Los Angeles

Bandits towel, then stare at the Pacific, willing the scene to calm my rattled nerves.

In the distance, a boat bobs along. Closer to the shore, a couple of towheaded toddlers cart buckets of sand for sandcastles. Off to the side, guys play volley-ball, spiking like they're trying out for the next *Top Gun*.

And all along the water, surfers and paddle boarders ride waves and paddle through them. Venice Beach is home for all sorts of board sports thanks to its mostly mellow crests. Neither are things I'll ever do, but I like to watch and to wade.

I stand and stretch. *Watch out, world. A top-notch toe-dipper is on her way into the Pacific.*

Leisurely, I make my way to the shoreline, letting the cool water kiss my feet. The early afternoon sun beats down on my shoulders as I wade in until the water reaches my waist. I freestyle for a few relaxing lengths, then my gaze catches on a paddle boarder two board lengths away, close enough for me to see the water bead on his carved abs.

Oh hello, eye candy.

I float on my back and indulge in the primo view.

That body will take a mind off a week of headaches, flat tires, and annoying exes—broad shoulders, carved abs, and a killer smile have that effect. Yup. Happy place, I am in you at last.

The hottie pushes his oar through the water,

gliding along a rolling crest of a wave, nice and smooth. Strong legs, big, delish arms, totally lickable abs—all his muscles rippling and glistening with ocean water.

I sigh. This is the kind of shirtlessness I can enjoy. Boarders *should* be shirtless.

But as I'm enjoying the scenery, another paddle boarder comes out of nowhere, dropping into Eye Candy's wave, and breaking a basic rule of the ocean road—don't jump in someone else's lane.

I pop upright, tensing, picturing dangerous scenarios unfolding. Ones that involve boards, and oars, and heads, and whacks.

The lanky guy loses his footing and tumbles backward off the board in a blur of limbs, hitting the water with a loud slap. The oar shoots from his hand on a fast track for Eye Candy. The former lifeguard in me shouts, "Heads-up!"

But not quickly enough.

Smack!

The oar connects with the back of the paddle boarder's noggin, and the hottie goes kersplat, face-first into the water. I cringe in sympathy as he's knocked under the sea.

I move as fast as I can, and as I reach the scene, the skinny guy surfaces and shakes his wet hair out of his eyes. Spotting his paddle board a few feet away, he swims off for it.

"You should be more careful," I chide.

All of twenty-nine, and I sound like a schoolmarm. Next, I'll be shouting *get off my lawn* at the neighborhood kids. But the guy doesn't even acknowledge me as he chases his board and, presumably, his oar.

A second later, the hottie pops up, brushing a hand along his face and over his wet hair. "Oof," he mutters and shakes his head like it's ringing.

"You okay?" I ask over the sound of the sea.

Blinking, he rubs the back of his head. His disoriented gaze is a little worrisome. I've got to get him out of the ocean. His board bobs near him, so I kick closer to it, then push it over to him. "Grab your board," I tell him, then I grab the oar.

He obeys, his strong arms resting on it. His are an homage to arm porn memes everywhere, but I shove aside my gawking to check in. "How are you doing?"

"I think I'll live," he says, his tone is a little dry. "Do you do this a lot?"

"Help out when a guy's been dropped in on?" I ask, and he gives a small nod. "I used to be a lifeguard. If I can help, I will."

"You're off-duty and you're checking on me," he says with a dreamy smile. "You're like the patron saint of paddle boarders."

And you have a body I'd like to worship, I want to say, but I don't, because *manners*. Besides, the man's clearly dizzy, and dizzy people don't belong in the water.

"I'm glad you're not feeling too bad," I say, gently

but firmly as I tip my head in the direction of the sand. "But maybe consider life on the shore for a few minutes."

"Not a bad idea. I hear there are fewer flying objects over there," he says, his lips twitching in a tiny grin as he paddles toward the shore.

"I don't know about that," I say as I swim alongside him, dragging the oar with me. "There are drones, frisbees, helicopters. Airplanes."

"Fewer flying oars," he corrects, with a bigger smile.

I smile too, since he seems no worse for wear. "That's one of its many selling points."

"I'm sold then." When the water is waist deep, he stands, picks up his board, and carries it as he wades out of the surf.

And...wow. That's a helluva backside.

I cannot stop staring. But in my defense...*his ass*.

He drops his board into the sugary sand, then sinks down next to it. There goes my butt view.

But the face view is *fine* too.

Swiping away dirty thoughts, I follow him out of the water and plop down beside him, setting the oar next to us. He looks familiar, but I can't place him. But it's Los Angeles. There's a ninety percent chance he's been in a commercial or is a background character in a movie.

"Lifeguard 101ing continues," I say, all bossy. "Let me see if you've got a cut."

"All right. Check me out." He goes with the flow, leaning forward so I can inspect his scalp. I peer closely, looking for any lacerations or scrapes. I sigh in relief when I find none.

"What's the diagnosis, doc?"

"Good news. Your skull is solid. No damage."

With a laugh, he raps the side of his head with his knuckles. "Like I tell my friends, this is a rock."

I laugh too. "Good thing, since that guy's oar had it in for you. But I *also* want to make sure you don't have a concussion. Would you humor me?"

With an easygoing shrug, he says, "Sure. I'll humor you." Then he quickly recites the correct date, time, and year.

Whoa. Someone has done this before. "Impressive."

"Why thank you," he says, a little devilish.

He answered the first question correctly, but I'm not done. If he goes back out there with a concussion, he could get seriously hurt. "Now, can you give me a series of numbers—"

"—backward?"

"Well, aren't you just a concussion protocol show-off?"

"Numbers. Serve 'em up." He wiggles his fingers. He doesn't sound dazed like he did in the water. His eyes are alight with mischief, and they hold mine.

Okay, cutie, you're on.

I fire off some tough-to-remember numbers. "Fine. 77, 119, 2056, 2, 34."

"34, 2, 2056, 119, 77," he says, smirking, "And...69."

My cheeks heat, and it's not from the warm sun overhead. But I stay in character. Like a game show host disappointed when a contestant guesses wrong, I say, "Damn. And you were so close too."

"Ah, but I aim for a little higher than *so close*. Give me another shot to go all the way."

Maybe I'm just flirt-finishing the test. But so be it. With a saucy shrug, I ask, "Now, can you repeat these five words in reverse order?" I give him five random nouns. "Boat. Cat. Shoe. Car. Book."

When he meets my gaze full-on, his hazel eyes are a little fiery and so familiar again.

Who is he? I blot out the rest of the beach, the volleyball guys, the families, the sound of kids racing into the waves, and really try to place him.

He licks his lips, hums, then takes his sweet time. "The one you were reading. McLaren, red please. Heels...*on you* in any color. Starts with a P and I'll say it when the lights are off. And a yacht," he says.

Forget the detective work. My belly is doing a sexy tango, and I can't quite think straight. This man is a fast talker with a dirty mind, and I am here for it.

"You win. A-plus on your test," I say.

He pumps a fist. "I love winning. Even if it means I have to get hit by a vindictive oar."

I laugh. "That'd be a good name for a band."

"I bet it *is* a name for a band."

"Everything is a name for a band these days," I add.

He snaps his fingers. "Rogue Wave Riders would be a sweet name too."

"They're playing at the Holy Cow Sunday night. They go on after Vengeful Kayaks, and then Angry Jet Skis closes the set," I say.

"We're so there," he says. He turns to me again, his expression shifting from joking to genuine. "Thanks again for the concussion check. Not gonna lie—avoiding concussions is a big life goal for me."

Now I'm curious. "Is that a risk in your line of work?"

"It's a risk in life," he says a little evasively, glancing away to survey the beach. Then he turns back to me and flashes a blindingly gorgeous smile. If it's a distraction ploy, it's effective, showing off his straight white teeth, his square jaw, his strong cheekbones.

And a little dimple in his chin that's so damn alluring.

Like the rest of him.

Oh. My. God.

Yes! That's the smile I see on TV. In his promo photos. When he thanks a reporter on the sidelines after a game.

I just never expected to bump into the quarterback of one of the city's football teams paddle boarding. Especially since most player contracts forbid water sports.

We're in the same freaking business. I work behind the scenes managing vendor contracts for the Los Angeles Bandits, the city's baseball team, and Drew Adams is on the field, leading the Devil Sharks to the end zone.

He's a rising star in the league, but in this city, especially in sports, you learn quickly to wait for someone famous to tell you who they are. So, I wave away the topic without letting on that I've finally recognized him. "Life is full of risks. Like the ocean. I'm sure that's a bumper sticker somewhere. I'm just glad you're doing better."

Another smile, this one grateful. "I appreciate you making sure I was okay." He gestures to the vast expanse of water, the scene of the fall, then offers his hand. "I'm..." He stops, seeming to swallow whatever he'd been going to say, and his eyes dart away and then back to mine. "I'm Andrew. Nice to meet you."

The media only ever refers to him as Drew. One quick glance around gives me the answer to the unexpected *Andrew*. The family with the towheads is two towels away from us. The volleyball guys are maybe twenty yards north. So far, he's been lucky that no one has seen him, and that no one caught his fall on camera.

Sure, it's also possible he doesn't want *me* to know who he is.

Two can play at this pretend game, and probably two should. It's just wiser, safer too, here in public.

"I'm Brooke," I say taking his hand. "But you can call me Beach Nurse. Wait, No. Surf Nurse is way cooler."

He laughs. "I was going to go with Surf Angel. But Surf Nurse works. Is that a new TV show you're on?"

"Yes. It's a reality show. I roam the beaches and save dudes in distress," I say as he lets go of my hand.

He growls. "Hey now. I wasn't in distress."

I tsk, but I'm teasing. "You were upside down underwater, Andrew."

"Fine, Brooke. I was totally a dude in distress and you're the surf damsel who saved me." He checks me out in my royal-blue seashell-patterned bikini, and he's not shy about it either. His eyes linger on my chest, then my belly, and then my legs. That little flutter turns into a full-blown swoop. If this is all today is—some eye-fucking—I don't mind at all.

Since I will take that and be thinking of him when I'm alone in bed tonight.

He clears his throat, his expression turning earnest, intense. "Thanks again for helping me out today."

That has a hint of "wrapping this up for a polite goodbye" to it. I'm a little disappointed because I've been enjoying his banter so much. The important thing, though, is he's not hurt and he had someone to look out for him.

"I hardly did anything," I tell him honestly. "I'm just glad you're fine."

Drew shakes his head adamantly. "You did a lot. You shouted *heads-up*. Escorted me to shore. Conducted a full-on test. And endured my innuendo," he says with a little twinkle in his eye.

"I wouldn't say your innuendo was a hardship," I say.

"I could so make a joke..."

"Oh please. Don't stop now. I need to hear this hardship joke."

"My innuendo is a...yacht," he says, then tosses his head back, clutching his belly. "Shoot. I'm sorry. That was bad. I'm going to need to *dock* myself some points."

I give him a stern look. "For being a joke show...*boat*."

"Exactly. You get it." He sits up straighter. "But what I want to say is"—he gestures to me—"this was worth getting hit for."

Oh.

Wow.

I'm not sure what to say. Chatting with him is such a welcome respite from punctured tires, OnlyFans requests, and promotions that passed me by. With Drew, I'm not the woman her ex wanted to interview.

I'm a lifeguard, a surf nurse, a damsel who saves dudes.

I'm the woman who was worth getting clocked by a paddleboard oar for.

"Thank you," I say softly. "I wish you didn't get hit. But I'm glad I was here to help."

"Me too," he says, then rubs his hand against the back of his head again. He winces. Uh-oh.

"Does your head still hurt?"

"Nah," he says, but it's the tough-guy answer.

"If you say so," I say, my tone saying *you're full of it*.

He dips his face. "Hurts a little," he admits, as if it costs him something.

"Let me take another look, okay?"

"Sure," he says, easily agreeing.

I kneel and move closer to him so I can run my fingers gently over his skull. "I hate to be the one to break this to you, but your head has got a funny shape," I whisper.

"Gee, thanks," he says, laughing as the sun ducks behind a stray cloud. "Really appreciate the compliment."

"I'm sorry," I deadpan as I run my palm up and down the back of his head. "You're probably used to women complimenting the shape of your skull. *Oh, it's so round, Andrew,*" I coo.

Amused, he shakes his head. "Known you for ten

minutes and I've already figured out you like giving me a hard time."

"Took you that long?"

He rolls his eyes. "Fine. Two minutes. The drone comment did it."

"Hmm. I'm pretty sure that was one minute into our fantastic new friendship," I say as the sun re-emerges from a cloud, warming my shoulders again. That feels fitting for this day—let the damn sun shine now. "But considering your *hardship* comment, I think you like it."

"I do like it," he admits, no sarcasm from him either this time.

When I drop my hand, I drop the games. "You do have a goose egg. You need to get some ice on it."

"Damn."

"Yeah, it's a big one," I say before it's too late.

He snickers. "That innuendo is on you. And you know what?"

"What?"

"You need to join me as I ice my head over there." He points to a bar on the corner of the boardwalk. It's tucked off to the side, and umbrellas offer privacy from passers-by and even from people in apartments nearby with views of the beach. He raises an eyebrow, and the invitation in his hazel eyes makes my stomach flip.

I try my best to fight off a grin. Really, I do.

But I fail, and I love failing, because it means this unexpectedly delightful moment isn't ending.

I rise, quickly tuck my Bandits towel in my mesh bag, and then tug on a purple tank top dress.

He whimpers. "I was enjoying the view," he says, as he stands.

The zip returns, speeding through me, settling between my legs. "Don't stop, then," I say.

"I won't," he says.

When I left my home this morning, I just wanted to forget the week from hell. Now, I'm on an impromptu date with a guy on the beach, and bad luck is the furthest thing from my mind.

Maybe things are starting to turn around.

Who needs sunshine and a book? Looks like my fantasies are about to become reality.

2

DON'T PUT THE PARROT BEFORE
THE UNICYCLE

Drew

If I'd known getting whacked upside the head would lead to a blonde beauty saving me, I'd have spent less time avoiding hits.

Currently, though, I'm avoiding the reality of my contract, my agent, and what's next in my career—all the questions that have chased me lately.

And I'm dodging reality my favorite way—in the company of a lovely lady.

"Let me drop my board off," I say when we reach the boardwalk.

"I'll grab a table," she says.

I'm parked nearby, so I'm soon loading the board into the back of a truck I borrowed from a friend, then I grab my phone and shades from the console and a hat from the front seat.

Shit. This hat has a Renegades logo on it. Understandable, since Carter plays for the San Francisco football team. But I can't wear a cap with our rivals on it in public. Or anywhere, for that matter. That shit would jinx my team, and we do not need more bad mojo.

Mostly, though, I kind of want to lie low with Brooke and just enjoy her company. I don't get recognized every day, but it happens often enough. Having a date is easier if I don't draw attention. I managed to paddle board without being spotted, and I'd like to keep my streak, so I need a lid.

Aha.

I spot another hat on the floor—light blue, with *Plays Well with Others* written on it. It's innocuous enough, so I grab it, adjust the back, then return to Brooke at the bar.

She arches a brow in curiosity, her eyes on my headwear. "Well, that's good to know," she remarks.

I adjust the brim. "I like to be direct."

"Clearly," she says. "And I appreciate the insider tip."

"More like an advertisement." I join her at the table, scooting my chair a little closer. Since...I do play well with others.

Brooke holds out a cloth napkin wrapped around

something bulky. "All right, Mister Paddle Board. I've got your ice pack right here."

Wow. She's...awesome. "Let the record reflect that you are the *only* person I want saving me from any future vindictive oars." I pick up the ice pack and press it against the back of my head, genuinely touched that she's so damn on top of things.

"I'm the picture of efficiency."

"And I'm the picture of being concussion-free. Check this out...77, 119, 2056, 2, 34. Also, boat. Cat. Shoe. Car. Book."

She scoffs. "I was expecting them backward."

My jaw drops in exaggerated outrage. "Woman, I remembered them fifteen minutes later. I want all the points."

She heaves a sigh of surrender. "Fine, you get sixty-nine points."

"Excellent." We settle in, and when the server swings by, my date orders a margarita and I opt for an iced tea, due to the recent head injury and all.

"All right. I have to know. Are you a big sister? You have some serious caretaker skills," I say.

"You figured me out. Although I believe Cara would call me a know-it-all, as well as a caretaker. And you? Any siblings?"

"Two half-sisters. They're nine. Mom re-married and, oops, twins."

Her eyes widen. "That's quite an oops."

"Sure is, but Mira and Sophie are the best. I'll be teaching them to paddle board soon."

When the server returns with our drinks, I lift my glass in a toast. "I'll drink to vindictive oars and angel nurses," I say.

She clinks back. "I'll drink to playing well with others."

"Goals," I say.

Brooke sets down her glass after a swallow and points to a big red parachute high over the water, where a woman rides the air currents, pulled by a boat below. "That might be something to consider," Brooke says. "I don't think there are too many vindictive parachutes in the sky."

"Noted. I'm a parasailing virgin, but it looks like fun." I sip my iced tea.

Her brown eyes widen at my comment, sparkling with surprise. "You should try it. Parasailing is so much fun, and it's like a cousin of paddle boarding."

I arch a brow. "Brooke, you sure about that? One, you hang on a swing. The other, you ride over waves."

"But you do one *in* the ocean and the other *above* it," she says with a sassy bob of her shoulder. "Ergo, cousins."

"Sounds like you're trying to win on a grammatical technicality," I tease, pressing the ice a little harder against my head. I want this bump gone, gone, gone.

Glancing away, she flicks some blonde strands off her shoulder. "Well, I'm a technicality kind of gal. It's sort of what I do all day," she says, and this is the part of the date where we make small talk about our jobs.

I should probably say at some point that I play pro ball. It'd be weird if I didn't 'fess up soon since I already play-faked my name, using Andrew instead of Drew. But when I introduced myself on the sand, I didn't feel like having the whole *I'm the quarterback who nearly got concussed in the ocean* conversation. Smooth, huh?

Honestly, I was stoked I hadn't been spotted. Don't want to end up on some podcast's compilation list of Dumb Shit Athletes Do. Even though my contract allows stand up paddle boarding, thank you very much. It's considered a safe sport with a low risk of injury. Lower than running.

But at least there's some privacy here in the corner of the boardwalk bar. "You're a technicality kind of woman, and I'm an active kind of guy," I say, easing into telling her who I am. "That's sort of what I do all day."

"Then you should try parasailing. Except...it's not active. You glide. But it is outdoors and fun," she says.

"I'll put it on my list of outdoor activities to try. Though I might try *that* first," I say, gesturing to the boardwalk where a guy rides a unicycle, a parrot perched on his shoulder.

"Do you have a parrot?" she asks.

"No, but I figure if I take to unicycling, I could get a parrot then," I say. "Don't put the parrot before the unicycle."

"As the saying goes," she says drily, then nods toward a pack of skateboarders in low-slung shorts tearing up the concrete. "But beware of dastardly skateboards when you ride."

"They're the real cousins to paddle boards." I lean back in my chair, soaking in the sun and the eclectic people. Farther down the path, someone plays the drums, beating out a hippy tune. This afternoon is everything I needed to reset. The laid-back vibe is a welcome contrast to practice this morning, which was tight and tense as our team managed to fuck up nearly every play. I was eager to get my mind off all the changes coming for me, so I came here to hit the waves.

But Brooke is a much better distraction than the Pacific. And so is that dude in a pink shirt and white shorts walking down the boardwalk on sky-high stilts.

"What do you think, Brooke? More or less daring than paddle boarding?" I ask, nodding toward the guy who's about ten feet taller than he should be.

She shudders. "Equally. And also on the list of things I won't ever try. I have a low tolerance for falling, splatting, or crashing onto the ground or into the sea. Hence, *reading*," she says, patting the book inside her mesh bag. "But I love to people watch, so Venice is perfect for *that* outdoor activity."

"Hands down. I live in Santa Monica, but there is no better place in all of Los Angeles for people watching than right here."

"That's why I live in this neighborhood. About ten minutes away. There's always something to do or see."

I study her closely, nodding a few times. "That tracks."

She knits her brow, clearly confused. "What tracks?"

"You living in Venice."

"Even though I don't have a parrot on my shoulder?"

"In spite of your parrot-free existence," I say with a smile, enjoying the hell out of the view of her. "You're fast on your feet, but you're not wound tight. You have a low-key vibe about you. And you're easy to talk to."

Brooke lifts her margarita glass, like she's toasting to me. "I'll drink to good conversations. You're easy to talk to, as well." I can't look away as she sips her drink. She has spectacular lips. I noticed her full red lips when we first started talking, even if my vision was a little fuzzy.

I'm glad I did fall victim to another guy's boarding fail because this moment right here is pretty damn great. Talking about the world around me with a beautiful, smart, caring woman rather than football, football, football is a welcome change. From...everything.

The last woman I dated was into me for the number on my back. The number of times Jenna asked me to pose for pics so she could tag me was too high to count. She was always talking about how she was Number Eight's *gal*, trying to parlay our relationship into more business at her lingerie store.

Sure, I'm all for high sales of lacy underthings for everyone, but that was not a way to make a guy feel wanted.

I have a lot to offer besides the position I play on Sundays, like a sense of humor, a big heart, and an even bigger dick. Bonus—I know how to use it.

Just saying.

One drink turns into two, and Brooke and I talk more about our favorite places in Los Angeles, and the best spots for people watching in the city.

The sun is sinking low in the sky when she asks, "And what's the story with the paddle boarding? Hobby? Passion? Are you new at it?"

"Admit it. I looked like a noob."

She laughs, then shakes her head. "No, actually. You seemed pretty good. Like you'd been doing it for a while."

"I took it up last year. I've been having a blast so far," I say, then knock back some iced tea. "What about you? Have you been reading for a while?"

"Did I seem like a natural reader?"

"Absolutely. I saw you on the sand before I went out," I reply, teasing. "You just had such an ease when turning the pages."

"Well, if you must know, I've been reading since I was five," she says.

"Whoa. I learned to read when I was five too," I deadpan.

"What a coincidence."

"We both like the beach and we both like to read," I say.

She lifts her drink. "But only one of us gets to drink a margarita."

I inch closer. "Maybe next time we both can." I leave that offer right there. Today is too much fun to be a one-time thing.

She licks the corner of her lips, then meets my gaze, her blonde locks falling over one eye. "Next time sounds like a good idea." Then she finishes her margarita and sets it down. "On that note..." She sits up straighter, gathering her things.

Wait.

What?

I wasn't done with this time. "Do you need to go?"

She blinks in slight confusion. "You said *next time*...I thought you meant you had to take off."

I shake my head, smiling. "Are inferences like technicalities for you? Something you look for a lot, Brooke?"

She shrugs sheepishly. "It's what I do. I'm an attorney, and I can't help but find loopholes, technicalities, and I'm *always* paying attention to inferences, Andrew."

Okay, if I'm hinting at a second date, and she's told me what she does for a living, I really need to come clean about my identity.

"Actually, everyone calls me Drew," I begin.

She lifts a brow, her lips curving up too. "So you want me to be like everyone?" Gently, she pushes her sandaled foot against my shin.

I push back, my flip-flop against the side of her calf. "Considering my mom is the only person who calls me Andrew, and she usually only says it when she's mad, I do want you to be like everyone."

She smiles. "Then I will be. And I'm still Brooke."

"Good," I say. I glance around. No one is close enough to hear. "So, Brooke, where do you—"

"We don't have to talk about work, Drew," she says gently, giving me an out. "Unless you want to. But if you don't want to, I'm kind of enjoying all this *not* talking about it. It was a helluva week."

Oh. Well. That never occurred to me—the *we can table it for later* possibility. But hell yeah. "Same here," I say, relieved. "Everything with work's up in the air for me."

Her eyes spark. "Me too. I was hoping something would happen with a job thing I wanted. A promotion. It didn't, and I came to the beach to escape."

"Same. I sort of don't know what's happening next." That hasn't changed, but I don't feel as frustrated as I did this morning.

She sits up straighter. "Exactly. It's weird to even think about going in tomorrow, or how I should act."

"It's tough, when your work future is unclear," I admit.

With a sage look, she says, "So, you're okay to skip the whole what-do-you-do conversation right now? We can discuss it later."

Later, as in after I take her home. Or later as in later in the week when I take her out to dinner. Either works for me.

"Then, it's a topic for next time," I say, then meet her brown-eyed gaze straight on. "You want to get out of here?"

"Now?" Her voice pitches up.

"Yes. Now. But if you'd rather not, that's cool. If you'd rather wait, next time is more than fine too."

She hesitates, seeming to weigh up my offer as she nibbles on the corner of her lips. "I don't want to take advantage of you, Drew. Your injury and all."

I toss my head back and laugh. "Honey, you're not taking advantage of me."

She rolls her eyes. "Your goose egg, I mean."

Like I'd let that stop me. "Want to check it?"

"Yes." Gently, she pushes the ice pack aside, brushing her palm over my head again. Her touch is reassuring. Caring. But also, arousing. She runs her long fingers over my head, and I'm picturing her hands tightening in my hair as I spread her legs and taste her.

Like maybe in the next fifteen minutes.

"What's the report?" I ask.

"I think your goose egg is history, Drew," she says.

That is excellent news. I lift my hand and tuck a strand of her soft hair behind her ear, then run my fingers down the strand. "Then, I'm good to go. Are you?"

Her eyes twinkle. "Let's get out of here."

3

ALL THE INNUENDO

Drew

I silently curse my board shorts. They don't hide a tent at all. But I'm both a gentleman and a strategist.

"After you," I say when we rise from the table. As she walks ahead of me, I recite a new passing route in my head. Boom. Five seconds to deflation.

There is nothing to send a dick downward like thoughts of work.

We stop on the street at Carter's truck, parked at the corner of the boardwalk with my board sticking out of the bed.

Brooke glances at the board, then looks at me. "I'm nearby, but if you'd rather drive, we can do that," she offers.

"I can handle a short walk."

"You're so tough," she says drily.

"That's me. Hardy. Able to withstand short walks from the beach on a beautiful day," I say, as I set a hand on the small of her back.

"You're not going to get a parking ticket, are you?"

I stop and tug her close until she's only a few inches from me. Sliding my hand through her hair again, I whisper, "If I do...*worth it.*"

Her cheeks pinken. Then a soft breath flutters past her lips. "Walk faster."

Ten minutes later, after a few turns here and there in the neighborhood, we reach her home, a cute little white bungalow. The porch teems with potted plants and flowers, as well as pizza coupons and takeout menus stuffed behind the mailbox next to the doorway. She turns to me and says in a professional tone, "Thank you. For the drinks and the speed walking."

Whoa. With her cool tone, she sounds like she's done. I might have whiplash.

But then a wicked grin spreads on her bee-stung lips. "Just kidding. I'm not done with you," she says as she unlocks the door then beckons me in.

"Good. Because I'm not done with you either, but for trying to fake me out I'm going to make sure you get all the innuendo you can handle," I say in a low, domineering tone.

"Oh. So me being sassy gets me—"

I close the distance and crush her lips with mine. A hard, firm kiss that lasts five seconds. "You were saying?" I ask innocently.

She stammers an *uhh*.

Yes. Kissed speechless. That's such a good look on her. I pull back, enjoying the view. She leans against the wall in her foyer, catching her breath. That pose shows off all her assets—the swell of her breasts in her tank top dress, her curvy hips, her strong legs.

Her parted lips too. She licks them and swallows. "As I was saying...*more* innuendo," she murmurs.

A rumble works its way up my chest as I step closer. This time, I take my sweet time, my hand traveling along her arm, her skin soft and inviting.

Goose bumps rise in my wake. "Do you know what I've been thinking about?" I ask.

"What's that, Drew?" Damn, my name sounds sexy on her lips.

I brush her hair off her shoulder, cataloging her reaction to my touch. The way she shivers. How she sways against me. The rush of breath on her lips. I bring my mouth to her ear and whisper, "What it would be like to kiss you...*everywhere.*"

"Oh God," she gasps, but I catch a flicker of worry in her eyes that makes me pause.

"Think you'd like that?" I ask.

She's quiet at first, then lets out a trembly breath. "I *think* so."

That doesn't sound as certain as I'd like. "You good with everything? You need me to stop?"

She hisses, pushes her hands against my chest, and grabs the neck of my shirt. "Do. Not. Stop."

Good. I don't fucking want to at all.

"Sounds like you need more kissing, then," I offer suggestively.

"I do."

I grab hold of her hip. "Good. Because I need a whole lot more of your gorgeous mouth."

My fingers roam up to her hair then rope through those thick blonde locks.

"Ahh," she murmurs, her eyes floating closed, her lush mouth waiting for me. There you go. Brooke just needs a little savoring, some sexy devotion to her pleasure.

I pull her body against me, enjoying the warmth of her sun-kissed skin and the smell of sand, surf, and sunshine in her hair.

I dip my mouth to hers, clasping her face in my hands. When I nip her bottom lip, she gasps. It's such an alluring sound.

I kiss her slowly, then tenderly. Then a little possessively. I travel across her lips, exploring, quickly learning her cues. She leans back against the wall, inviting me to crowd her, asking me to lead.

Next, I kiss her intently. A deep, passionate kiss that's a recipe for how I want to fuck her.

Every sigh, every moan tells me she'd like a man to take care of all her needs.

Well, she came to the right beach and found the right guy.

Afternoon delight, here we come.

Brooke presses her sexy body to mine as I claim her mouth in another consuming kiss that intensifies until I'm devouring her lips. She moans and murmurs and loops her hands around my neck, tugging me closer. I leave a path of kisses along her jaw, her cheek, her neck. Her skin tastes so good, I could spend hours here, nibbling, kissing, biting. Maybe next time. For now, I nip her earlobe.

She murmurs, a long, sexy, lingering noise. "Mmm. That feels so good."

"You deserve to feel good," I whisper in her ear.

As I flick my tongue over the shell of her ear, her pitch rises, turning into that gorgeous gasp a woman makes as she gets turned on.

Grabbing her hips, I tug her closer. "Those little sexy noises drive me wild," I tell her.

"I want you to make me shout," she whispers like she just voiced something so daring, so out of the ordinary.

"Then we better get started."

"Yes. Now. Please."

I hoist her up and toss her over my shoulder. "Where's your bedroom?"

She points down the hall and, with a smile in her voice, says, "That way."

I carry her to her bed, ready to give her all the innuendo and then some.

4

THE THING IS…

Brooke

Drew drops me on the mattress and settles between my legs, his hands inching up my thighs.

I want this so much but I have to tell him something. Even though my skin is tingling so much that it'd seem I'll have no trouble going over the cliff, I know I will, and it'll be awkward. I don't want to be awkward with Drew. I like him too much already. I push onto my elbows and say, "I need to tell you something."

I sit up, my chest tightening with nerves.

His eyes flash, clearly wary I might drop some truth bomb on him.

Quickly, I try to smooth over the awkwardness. "I can't come through oral."

He blinks but quickly covers his surprise. "Oh. Okay," he says. Then, after a pause to process the info, he says, "You never have?"

I shake my head. "Never."

He sits back on his knees, his gaze going thoughtful. My heart crashes. I ruined a sexy moment. "Also, I don't orgasm easily through sex," I say, then wince.

Way to go, Brooke.

God, I want to muzzle myself.

But we already agreed to hit pause on the work convo. I don't want to hit pause on the *I'm complicated in bed* convo. Because he'll figure it out in a few minutes anyway.

Drew leans forward, grabs my chin, and whisks a soft kiss across my lips. "But do you like sex?"

Screw it. I rip off the Band-Aid. "Sometimes. When it's good. But it hasn't always been good."

It hasn't been good at all, actually.

But I keep that to myself. I don't want to sound too complain-y.

Drew nods again, taking in the info. "So, you're not...I'm not sure what the right word is...uninterested in sex?"

I whip my head side to side. "Oh, I'm very interested. Sometimes, it's a sex fiesta up here," I say, tapping my temple.

He smiles wickedly. "Excellent. I have that same situation going on upstairs too."

"I think about it a ton. I like the idea of oral. In

my fantasies, I come that way," I say, enjoying telling him that. I want him to know I'm...curious.

He reaches for my left ankle, absently stroking it with his thumb. The light touch sends small zings of pleasure up my leg. "Then you're not opposed to a guy going down on you?"

"God, no. I have zero opposition."

"And you are, in fact, in support of it," he offers.

"Yes. I love the idea," I admit.

When he brushes his palms over my knees, then traces the space behind them, I shiver.

Have I ever shivered from that before? I'm not sure.

"But you don't love the reality of it," he says, his hand traveling farther up my thighs, drawing maddeningly light strokes on my skin.

My eyes close for a few seconds as I sink into the fizzy sensations. "I haven't loved it. I want to, but I haven't."

I'm not sure why I'm comfortable telling Drew when he's a stranger. But perhaps that's why. Because our connection is sexual. Drew mentioned a *next time*, but there are no guarantees. There is only *this time*.

And if that's all there is, then I want it to be amazing.

With a soft murmur, Drew nods, his hands dancing closer to my bikini bottoms. Then, he shifts directions and inches down my body, watching me as he goes. "Let's make a deal."

I laugh with anticipation. "What kind of deal?"

He slinks lower, reaching the end of the bed, and then runs those big, warm hands over my skin. He dips his face to my ankle, kissing me there.

I wriggle from the shot of bliss.

He doesn't answer my question as he moves to my other ankle, dusts a gentle kiss there, then travels upward, kissing my calf, my shin, my knee.

I tremble.

He lavishes the same attention on my left leg, moving up my thighs.

"Ohhh," I murmur as he caresses me with tender, open-mouthed kisses until he reaches my center.

Then, he looks up, looking pleased but not cocky. "So, here are my terms."

"Right. Sure. What are they?"

"You let me keep trying *this* till you're shouting my name," he says.

Oh, fuck me.

I heat up all over. My core aches exquisitely.

"That sounds like a terrific offer," I murmur.

"Good," he says, then whip-fast, he tugs my bikini bottoms down, pushes up my dress, and settles between my thighs.

"Mmm," he says gazing at me. "You have such a pretty pussy."

His dirty mouth is such a rush. I love how that word sounds on his lips. How carnal.

Drew gazes at me like he's trying to decide how he wants to go down on me, then he sinks between my thighs, slides his hands under my ass, and brings me to his mouth.

And *wow*.

I groan from the first contact. He's moaning and he's only just started. He's French kissing me slowly and squeezing my ass tenderly, and I feel like dessert.

I thought I'd feel like a project. A problem to solve.

But Drew goes down on me like he wants to learn every detail of my body and catalog all of my wants, my needs.

My dirty desires.

They aren't complicated. But they are rarely fulfilled.

I've grown accustomed to spectacular sex in my head, mediocre sex in my life.

But right now, with this man's face between my legs, his mouth murmuring against my flesh?

Nothing is mediocre.

I melt into the bed as he kisses and licks. Then he stops for a second, looks up at me. His mouth glistens. His eyes sparkle. "Bet you'd like it more if you grabbed my hair," he suggests, his eyes drifting to my hands by my sides.

Oh. Sheesh. I'm a piece of work. "Sometimes I

don't know what to do with my hands," I say, feeling a little foolish.

"I'll show you what I like then. That work for you?" he asks.

Oh, God. *Yes.* No one has said that before. "Please," I rush out.

He reaches for my hands, returns his mouth to my center, then curls my fingers around his head.

With a long, slow, tantalizing lick, he makes a show-don't-tell case for spending the day between my thighs. Then, he says, "Grab my head hard. Run your fingers through my hair. Pull me close. Push me away. Do whatever the fuck you want." With his eyes locked on mine, he lowers his voice more. "Use my face to get off."

Holy fuck.

I sizzle from head to toe. No one has ever spoken to me like that. So direct, so dirty.

I tighten my grip around his head, then close my eyes. "Do that thing again. What you just did," I whisper.

"Like this?" he asks seductively, then takes all the luxurious time in the world licking me.

Up, down, over and again.

I grip tighter, tug him closer. Only once does he break his pace to say, "That's right, Brooke. Do whatever you want. Fuck my face like this," he urges.

Tingles shoot up my legs and coil in my belly where a tight, hot pulse races faster, faster. And it feels so good, like I'm so close. I want to shout and cry. I want to give in to this moment.

But *what if?*

What if it doesn't happen?

I stay quiet, too afraid to let go.

Even though I'm on the cusp, there's no way I'll reach the end.

I wrap my hands tighter around him, but I don't pull him closer. I push him off.

He looks both concerned and drunk on me. "Everything okay?"

"Yes, but I'll have a better shot if you flip me over and fuck me so hard I can't think."

He stares at me with his jaw hanging open as if he can't believe his luck. "This is the best day ever."

Let's hope so.

Quickly, I find a condom in the nightstand then set it on the bed so I can tug off his shirt. I roam my hands all over him, a quick exploration. "Your chest...wow. Just wow," I say, then I want to get to know his arms too.

But he grabs my wrists and stops me. "When my face was between your thighs, you were afraid you wouldn't come, right?"

I close my eyes, then nod. "Yes."

Drew kisses my cheek. "Next time, honey. Next time you'll let me finish," he says in a gorgeous seduction that makes me want to sign up for that next time even though there's no guarantee I'll get over the cliff *this* time. What if I don't?

But I stop thinking when Drew stands at the edge of my bed, unties his shorts, and lets them fall to the floor.

My mouth waters.

His cock is gorgeous. Screw thinking. I want to feel.

5

TERMS OF ENGAGEMENT

Drew

I strip off her tank dress, undo her bikini top, then cup her breasts.

I could play with these beauties for a long time. But she needs to get lost in the feelings now. "Turn around, hands on the bed. And lift your ass," I order.

She obeys, spinning around, lifting her ass, and waiting.

"Mmm," I say, gliding my hand over her cheeks. "This is my favorite view. But I'd like it a little better if I were balls deep in you."

She shudders. My sweet afternoon delight loves dirty talk. I take a few seconds to open the condom, roll it on, then rub the head of my cock against her heat, my own temperature spiking.

She may worry about coming. She may have a hard time reaching the end. And I may never give her an orgasm.

But I'm going to try like hell. "Were you this wet back at the bar?" I ask.

"Yes. I was turned on just being near you," she whispers.

"You made me so fucking hard just by flirting with me," I say, then I grab her hips. "Let me do all the work, honey. I've been thinking for the last two hours about how to fuck you."

"Show me," she murmurs.

"I will." I ease out, swivel my hips, and sink in, filling her and indulging in this moment deep inside her. "You want it hard? Slow? You want me to smack your ass? Name it, honey."

"Deep. Just deep. I love it when…"

"When I fill you up," I say, finishing for her as her speech spins into a dirty moan.

Then, another.

A loud groan.

A blissed-out sigh.

Soon, she's hitting a fast pace of cries. She's close, and I don't want her to lose it again. As I fill her and fuck her, I find her swollen clit, and I rub. Just the right pressure. Just the right touch.

My mission? Overwhelm her with pleasure so she can't think.

And I don't relent. I keep the rhythm of hard, deep thrusts. Focused swirls of my finger.

Most of all...words.

So hot, so tight, so good.

I'm close to the edge too.

Soon, I'll lose control.

But I hold on till she tips over, her sounds turning into a gorgeous cry of *oh God, oh God, oh God.*

Once, twice, then countless times as she comes.

I follow her there, rocking into her, my own release blurring out the world.

When at last we both come back to earth, I lean over her and kiss her shoulder. "Don't think for a moment that I forgot the terms of our deal. I have yet to make you scream my name while my face is between your thighs."

She laughs. "So I get another chance."

"We both do."

* * *

Some things women do amaze me. Like that bra trick where they take it off from under their clothes. A bit of wiggling then *voila*—free-range boobs.

I'm equally floored that Brooke can throw together a meal after such epic sex. My brain is still coming back online, and she's whipping up a risotto dish in a frying pan, sautéing mushrooms and asparagus too.

"How did you do that?" I gesture in awe to the goodness on the stove, crackling and sizzling in her cute little kitchen. Yellow walls make the place warm and inviting, and the evening sun streams through the windows.

"Do what? Cook?"

"More like put together a recipe that quickly. You chopped the asparagus and mushrooms in no time," I say, scratching my jaw, trying to put two and two together in my post-orgasm haze. "Honestly, I'm not sure I'm speaking in complete sentences after that. I'm still feeling a little sex drunk."

She pats my shoulder. "You're managing. I'm following."

"Must do sex again," I grunt, caveman style.

"Okay, you're de-evolving," she says with a laugh.

"Sex and tacos. Must have sex and tacos next time," I continue.

"Well, that's clear."

I go back to normal. "Forgive my appetite. Great sex makes me extra hungry," I say, coming in closer to drop a tender kiss on the back of her neck. She smells like *us*.

She leans against me, seeming to savor the soft kiss too. "You're forgiven," she whispers.

But then she returns her focus to the food. As she pushes the veggies around with a spatula, she says, "Want to know my secret? To tossing the veggies in the pan so quickly?"

"I really do."

She drops her voice to a stage whisper. "The veggies were pre-chopped."

I whistle. "Damn, woman. And that's a good trick but it doesn't detract from the brainpower required to remember you had them. You are a surf angel rock star attorney goddess," I say as she takes the frying pan off the heat, setting it on a trivet.

I steal another kiss. Her post-sex scent is like a hit of sunshine on a rainy day. Then I steal another. And now, one more on her ear.

"Drew, you have to behave. I want to season the veggies," she says as I kiss her collarbone.

"That means I have to stop kissing you?" I ask, appalled at such blasphemy.

"Yes. For twenty seconds."

"Fine, fine. Focus on the food instead," I say, faux dismissively.

She turns around and gently swats my arm. "Your stomach was growling. You're the one who was hungry."

"You made me hungry! And I have no regrets."

Laughing, she shakes some salt and pepper and rosemary on the risotto, then tells me to grab a beer or a LaCroix from the fridge. Don't want to overstay my welcome, so I pick the LaCroix, snagging one for her as well, then we sit at the counter and dig in.

Holy shit. Brooke can cook. I groan in appreciation.

"Oh please," she says. "It's just from a bag from Trader Joe's."

I scoff. "Doesn't make me like it less. This is tasty."

I appreciate the grub—food and I are good friends—but I like the company even more. So much, I don't want to go. But I should. Soon.

Very soon.

I just want to lock in another date first.

I clear my throat. We agreed to talk about work later, and now *is* later. "I feel like I played hooky today. Sunday always feels like a workday to me. I'm used to working pretty much every Sunday during the fall. I play football," I say, then take another bite, relieved to finally be forthcoming about who I am.

She smiles softly. A hint of a secret lingers in her grin. "You're the quarterback."

I pause, my fork midair. "Um, yeah." I feel like I hit my head again. I wasn't expecting her to know, so I add stupidly, "For the Los Angeles Devil Sharks."

She squeezes my arm, smiling again. "And you had a hell of a season. One of those where-did-he-come-from years. Your passer rating was in the top eight last year, and your touchdowns thrown were in the top six."

I set the fork down so I don't drop it from shock. "You know all that?"

"Drew, I love sports. I work in the sports business too. And to be clear, I didn't help you because of that." She fidgets with her napkin. "I didn't even realize who you were until we'd been sitting on the sand and talking for a while."

Oh, shit. I didn't mean she has to justify herself. "It never entered my mind that you only saved me because I'm a player," I say, grabbing her hand from my arm, threading my fingers through hers. "I was surprised you knew, not annoyed. Also, kind of amazed at the depth of your knowledge."

She lets out a long breath. "Good. It felt weird knowing who you were and not saying anything, but it seemed like you didn't want anyone to recognize you. So, I went along with it."

I grimace, worried I might have come across as foolish as I feel now. "Did I sound like I assumed you were a football groupie?" God, I hope not. "I never want to sound like that kind of sexist jackass. Like I think I'm a star or that I assume all women want…" I can't even finish the sexist thought. "I swear I don't think that."

She shakes her head, reassuring me. "I've worked in this field for five years now. I understand players value their privacy. I wanted to make sure you had yours. I figured you had your reasons."

This woman. She's some kind of luck, falling into my lap. And the next time I see her, I am going to feed her tacos and go for a walk on the beach and then fuck her to six, maybe seven orgasms. "Have I mentioned you're a rock star? Because you are."

But enough about me. There's still so much I want to know about her. "Do you do sports law? My agent is a lawyer, and he's pretty badass. I could see you wearing a cape and flying in to save clients from scuffles, like you did with a dude in distress in the water."

"My job is not nearly as exciting as being an agent or a quarterback. I'm an attorney for the Los Angeles Bandits," she says, naming the city's baseball team. "I work on vendor contracts."

"I love baseball. It's the second-best sport, and those guys are having a great season," I say, digging into the dish for another bite.

"They are. We're hosting the All-Star Game next season, so that's keeping me busy, working on deals in advance of that."

We chat a bit more about baseball as we finish the meal. I help her clean up, and when we're done, I reach for her hand to pull her close. "That was amazing. Let's do this again—the beach, the drinks, the sex, the meal..."

"But no angry oars next time," she says.

"I'll do my best to avoid them," I say.

She purses her lips like she's holding back a smile. "I had the worst week. This has been...such an unexpectedly nice end to it."

"Good. Then I'm thinking tacos and ice cream and you holding me to my deal. How's Thursday night?"

"I'm in. For all of it," she says.

It's a promise—another time. Another night.

"There's a great place about a mile from here. Tacos Are Life." I grab my phone from my back pocket. Takes my text app longer than usual to open, but when it does, I say, "Give me your number."

"Yes, sir." She snags her own phone from the kitchen counter and opens her texts. "Hmm. I'll enter you as My O Dealer."

Ooh. She's a fun one to keep up with. "I'll have to enter you as...IOU."

She laughs. "Yes. You do, Drew."

I send her a message on the spot. *Thursday night. Tacos Are Life. Seven-thirty. It's a deal.*

She writes back with *I can't wait...for the tacos.*

With a kiss goodbye, I take off, counting the hours until the end of the week.

* * *

At sunrise the next morning, I'm peeling off miles of the beach on fleet feet, powered by the morning-after mojo of a sexy night and the promise of another one soon.

Carter keeps pace with me. At this hour, we pretty much have the beach to ourselves, the lapping of the waves the soundtrack to our workout.

"This is the best run I've had in ages," I say.

"You got laid last night," my college friend observes.

I crack up then meet his gaze. "That obvious?"

He gives an *I-know-you-so-well* nod. "The only thing that makes a man this chipper about running is sex. Plus, you were a surly mofo yesterday when you picked up my truck. I don't think the waves could namaste you like a hot date would. Was she a swipe right?"

"No!" I say, punching his arm. I'm still kind of amazed I met a fantastic woman randomly. "Can you believe I met her IRL?"

He snarls. "Dude. You're making me jelly. That still happens?"

"Evidently. I know you're the king of the dating apps and all, but I am all for meeting a woman without the smoke and mirrors of the Internet," I say.

Carter is easy to talk to about dating. He not only loves it, but he's a spokesperson for romance. His partnership with the Date Night app is a perfect match.

"So I was paddle boarding," I begin, then I tell him the rest of the story of meeting Brooke, ending with, "And I'm going to see her Thursday."

"You suck," he mutters.

I give a smug smile. After Jenna, I'm going to take this piece of good-dating luck and clutch it tight. "I know."

"Seriously. You meeting a woman on the beach is

like finding a Benjamin in the dryer," he says, then glances at his digital watch. He jerks his gaze back in the direction of Santa Monica.

I wheel around, and we start the return leg of our roundtrip jog.

"Are you spending a lot of time looking in laundry machines for extra dough, Carter? If you need a loan, just tell me."

He flips me the bird. "Why do I even hang around with you when I'm in LA? You walk ass-backward into great sex and then, without any pain or suffering, land a date with a woman you like."

"Aww, tell me how hard your life is. Is it still rough after winning the Super Bowl?"

He hums, a long, satisfied sound, then he raises his finger and scratches his jaw, showing off one of his fat rings. "Come to think of it, that was a sweet end to this season. An encore," he says.

Some guys have all the football luck.

"There. So I will enjoy my dating luck, while I try to figure out what the fuck is going on with my football team. The general manager has been cutting guys left and right. Practice yesterday was miserable. No one knows what kind of shake-ups there could be before the season kickoff. And it starts soon."

Carter knows this. He splits time between Los Angeles, his hometown and where his family still lives, and San Francisco, where he plays for the Renegades. He's in town since his team doesn't have practice today, but he'll be heading back later this week as we get ready for the regular season to start.

"I feel for you," my buddy says, then claps my shoulder. "I mean it. Even with my two rings, I still feel for you."

"Jackass," I mutter, then we trash talk the rest of the way to the Santa Monica Pier. When we get there, we head toward Ocean Avenue, where I spot a familiar figure at a café at the edge of the beach. He sits facing our direction, arms crossed loosely, almost as if he's been expecting us.

I slow my pace, pointing. "Dude, is that our agent?" What the hell is Maddox doing here?

"Whoa. He knows everything," Carter whispers in admiration. "Maddox knew exactly where we'd be on a Monday morning. He's a fucking genius."

I'll say. The man is ridiculously good at his job and never stops working. Hence, his tracking us down at seven-thirty. The guy is the picture of cool and calm. Impeccably dressed in slacks and a tailored shirt, he sips a cup of espresso as he waits and smiles in satisfaction as I reach him and stop a few paces away.

"I thought I might find you here when you didn't answer your phone," he tells me.

I grab for my cell in my pocket, spotting the missed call. Weird. I didn't think I turned off the sound. "Guess I put it on silent," I say.

Carter smacks my arm. "You missed a call from me last night too."

I shoot him a sneaky look. "I wouldn't say I *missed* it." Then I turn to Maddox again. "Good to see you."

Maddox gives an easy shrug. "Fortunately, I knew how to find you."

"I'm a creature of habit," I say with a smile, eager to find out why he's parachuted into my morning workout.

Carter thumps our agent on the back. "So, Super Agent, are you here to see him or are you stopping in to see your favorite client while he's in town?"

"I love all my children equally," Maddox teases.

"You don't have to say that just to make Carter feel better," I say, then I cut to the chase. "What's the story?" I point my thumb at my buddy. "Unless it's top secret, Carter can stay. I'll probably tell him anyway."

Carter cups the side of his mouth. "News flash— Drew got laid last night."

"Hey now. It was more than sex. I have a date with her." I

don't want to sound like a playboy.

Maddox just grins, shaking his head like we're a couple of clowns. Which, admittedly, we are. "Glad you met someone you like, Drew." His smile disappears, and he's suddenly serious. "I have big news, Drew. Now, let's talk."

6

ONE HORCHATA LATTE FOR ME

Brooke

I yank open the kitchen cupboard in Cara's apartment on Thursday morning and stare at the nearly bare shelves.

"How do you *not* have coffee?" I whine.

"There's this thing called coffee shops," she calls breezily from the other room. Her shoes clack against the tiles as she marches into the kitchen, her blonde hair swishing in a high ponytail. "You go in, order your drink, and voila. The barista serves it."

"But you need coffee for *meeeee*," I say, more dramatic than I need to be. But hell, I need to be.

"Tell you what. I'll splurge and take you out for a coffee on the way to class. How's that?" she asks.

"I can't let you do that. The fact you offered,

though, is proof I don't deserve you." I drag my hands through my hair, exasperated.

She comes up behind me. Rubs my shoulder. "Hello? Earth to Brooke. Coffee is not cause for drama. I may be broke, but I can afford a coffee. But maybe it's not coffee you want?"

I want to go back in time to Sunday and not give Drew my number. Then I wouldn't be wondering why I haven't heard from him.

Not a single text since he left my home. Since we made a date for tonight. His silence wouldn't be a problem except that on Monday, my boss told me he needed me to attend this charity event that went until seven p.m.

I texted Drew asking to meet me later than we'd planned, but he never replied. That was three days ago. We're supposed to meet *tonight*.

He's ghosted me, I know it.

Why, universe, why did he keep up the ruse all of Sunday night?

Oh, right. He wanted to get laid.

I take a deep breath. *Breathe in. Breathe out. Let go of my frustration.* "I think I woke up on the wrong side of the week," I tell my sister.

"It's that guy, right?" Cara asks as she grabs her phone from the counter and tucks it into the back pocket of her skinny jeans.

I look at her in surprise. I'm that obvious? "How did you know that was why I was annoyed?"

She laughs knowingly. "Because the second he left the other night, you called to tell me what an amazing time you had."

Of course, I'm that obvious. Like a starry-eyed teen, I gushed about Drew. So much for the tough girl routine I try to foster at work. Outside of the office, one fantastic night turned me into a marshmallow.

My throat tightens with a stupid lump. "I feel so foolish. I was so sure we'd have a second date. And I wanted that," I say, a sob threatening my composure. "After the work thing and everything…"

But I press the brakes. I don't want to indulge in a pity party over a man I had a one-night stand with.

I'm here this morning for Cara—to drive her to class on my way to work since her car is in the shop. She's finishing her master's degree to become a special education teacher, and I couldn't be prouder of my little sister.

I swallow the threat of tears and raise my chin. "Forget it. It's no biggie. Tell me more about what classes you have today," I say as we walk to the door.

She tugs gently on my hair, something she always did when she was little. "I will, but I can't thank you enough for driving me. My car is asking for a knuckle sandwich these days." She holds up her fist to demonstrate what she wants to do to her little Honda.

"You're not that far from me, and your class is on

my way in." I like helping her, and the reality is, I'm her third parent.

We head down the steps of her building and slide into my car, then pull into sluggish morning traffic. But we don't have far to go—just a couple miles.

As I slow at a light, I hear Cara hum to herself, something brewing in her big brain. That's my sister —always thinking. Revisiting. Trying again.

With a laugh, I say, "Spit it out."

She screws up the corner of her lips, then looks at me, her blue eyes intense. "You *could* call him."

I answer with a scoff.

"You could, Brooke," she insists.

"I'm not going to chase a guy who doesn't want to be chased," I say as the light changes and I hit the gas.

I still can't believe I misread Drew Adams so badly. But he played me, and that's just part of modern dating.

Ever the optimist, Cara goes on, "Maybe something legit happened. You really liked him, and you guys had a good connection. You're a confident, single woman, and you don't need to wait for a man to call you or respond to a text. There could be a simple explanation for him not answering your text." She snaps her fingers. "Like he dropped his phone in the shower."

I crack up. "Why on earth would he be using his phone in the shower?"

"Watching the news obviously," she says. "He's so worldly and concerned about the state of global affairs that he watches the news in the shower."

"And then he slipped and broke his phone?"

"It was a very intense news story." Her eyes widen as she embellishes the tale. "Or maybe the phone shielded his fall!"

"Or maybe you're reading too many news stories yourself, Miss NewsHound. You love little facts about all the terrible things that happen."

"No, I love to be prepared. And that's why I always have bathmats on the tiles, since lots of accidental injuries occur in the bathroom. Things get slippery in the shower. All I'm saying is it's possible there's an explanation for him not texting."

"Explanations like that only happen in the movies. Real life is men saying they'll do one thing, then doing another," I say crisply, gripping the wheel tighter, focusing on the road. Men need to stay in the rearview mirror. I have to learn my lesson from Sailor. "Look. It's all for the best. It's going to be a busy season. The more I focus on doing my best at the office, the greater the chance I can have at landing the next job."

"Have you decided what to do yet? About the work thing?"

I've cooled off since last week. I'm determined to impress Stephen and win the next promotion. "It's a small world, and I think I'll just keep trying hard with the Bandits," I say, but then I flash her a devilish smile. "But obviously I'll keep my ear to the ground for better opportunities."

"Obviously. You're always strategic. And I love that plan," she says.

I reach her building on campus. "Love you. Get out of here."

She leans across the console to give me a sloppy kiss on the cheek and then grabs her bag and heads out.

I watch her go, feeling warm and fuzzy as she heads into the building. Proud too. We spent many nights hunting down scholarships in her field. She nailed a handful and only has to pay a few thousand dollars a year. Loans are no fun. I'm still saddled with my law school loans, though I've been steadily chipping away at them. Another couple of years and I can pay them off.

Then, maybe I can help my parents out. Dad's a high school football coach. Mom is a bank teller, and the last recession took a bite out of their retirement funds. I'd love to take care of them in little ways.

But first things first. Pay off the rest of my loans.

And I can do that as long as I keep this job, which means focusing on work—not the date who's ghosted me.

I tap the gas and take off for the Bandits facility, ready to put Drew in the rearview mirror.

* * *

Sports have been a part of my life since I was a kid, thanks to my dad. We had some of our best father-daughter chats while throwing a ball in the backyard. He'd share his playbook for upcoming games, and I'd pepper him with questions. I analyzed everything about how football was played, fought, and won. I learned the formations, the types of coverage, and when to go for a forward pass, a screen pass, or a play-action pass.

Sometimes, he'd ask me what to do in an upcoming game, and I'd weigh in with suggestions based on the opponents and their style of play—their skills at running and passing, or whether they were defensive-minded, and so on. Dad would take all my feedback seriously, even though with a winning record of over thirty years, he hardly needed my help.

I'm still grateful for those chats now. Being a lawyer is all about strategy, and those sideline talks with Dad made me a very good lawyer.

My work lets me apply my questioning mind to something I love—sports.

When I arrive at the ballpark, I head to the executive suites, saying hello to my colleagues along the way.

There's Nancy in publicity, who wants to know when I'm going to do an interview with Sailor.

Felipe in college scouting, who watches all of Sailor's videos.

Abby in analytics, who has a crush on Sailor.

Before I reach my office, my phone buzzes with a message from Stephen. *Brooke, can you come to my office when you arrive? I picked up lattes.*

I study the note with suspicion. After all, this is the man who sent flowers when he passed me over for a promotion.

With dread coiling in my gut, I walk the plank to his office.

Even though I was frustrated with my job last week, I don't want to lose it. I can't afford to lose it.

I reach his door. It's ajar, and he's typing on his phone from behind his desk, expressionless.

"Good morning, Stephen," I say cheerily.

Putting his phone down, he looks up. "Come in," he says, laissez-faire as always.

I step inside the pit of doom.

Taking his time, he stands, walks around his desk, and grabs a cup. "Remembered you liked horchata lattes," he says. Most of the time, the man talks in phrases. "When you indulge, that is." He taps his temple. "Filed every team member's coffee prefer-ence. Comes in handy."

Is that the secret to being an EVP? Memorizing the staff's coffee orders? Is that handy when you need to fire them?

"Stopped by the Cuban café near the ballpark

and picked some up for you," he says and holds the cup out for me.

"Thanks," I say tentatively, taking it.

He takes one for himself from his desk too. "Try it."

I lift the cup and down the hatch it goes. And wow. That is tasty, warm, and cinnamon-y.

And damn him for his well-honed strategy. Making an employee feel good before you drop the hatchet.

"Sit," he says, gesturing to a chair. I obey.

He parks himself in the chair across from me. "Wanted to take you out to lunch to tell you this," he says, and I brace myself. It's coming.

Oh yes, it's coming.

"But...I couldn't wait till lunch. So horchata it is," he says, then his gray eyes dance and, wait. Is that a hint of a smile too, to go along with a full sentence? "The reason you didn't get the promotion is...we have a brand-new job for you instead. And you're the only one I trust to do it."

A few full sentences.

"I am? You do?" Wait. No. I shouldn't be speaking in question marks. I clear my throat. "I can't wait to hear about it."

"We're adding new responsibilities to your plate. Along with a hefty raise," he says, then shares the dollar amount.

I purse my lips so I don't drop my jaw.

But holy ovaries. That's a twenty percent increase. It's like a hazard-pay level raise. "That sounds terrific. And what are the added responsibilities?"

Stephen beams, something he rarely does. "We want you to handle legal work for both the baseball and football teams that Carlisle Enterprises owns."

I nearly jerk back in my chair. I did not see that coming. Of course I know Elizabeth Carlisle also owns the Los Angeles Mercenaries, but the day-to-day operations are run separately. "That would be great," I say, trying to strike a balance between gobsmacked and appreciative. I'm not the overly effusive type, even though I want to overly effuse right now.

Because I love football.

And responsibility.

And I really like more money.

Stephen exhales, as if relieved I said yes. I mean, how the hell was I going to say no to that?

Fine, the Mercenaries are a bit of a poster-child team for bad boys, but I won't be managing the players or their hard-partying reps. That's for the press department and the GM, frankly, or should be.

"When can I start?"

"Today," he says.

I sit up straighter. "I'm ready."

"Great. As part of your new responsibilities, we want you to review all the press releases and statements for both teams, especially with the heat the

Mercenaries have been under due to the, how shall we say, player fuckups in the last year."

And I guess I will be helping manage the bad reps after all. But in a hands-off way.

"Of course. It'll be wise to have legal eyes on those," I say.

"You're my best eyes, Holland," he says, using my last name. "Tonight at the charity event, I'll introduce you to the players you'll be working with."

I fasten on a smile. "I'll be ready."

This takes the sting out of a guy ghosting me before our second date.

I didn't get the promotion. I got an even better job.

I spend the rest of the day getting up to speed on the Mercenaries, but I'm pretty dialed in already as a fan. Also, as someone who works for the parent company, it'd be hard to miss any of the notorious scandals the team has been involved in.

The sports gossip sites had a field day with the Mercenaries last season. The team served up a buffet of juicy news all year long. Spin the roster like a lazy Susan and grab a drug or sex scandal when it stops.

A defensive back totaled his Ferrari while coked up. The nose guard trashed a hotel room doing speed. The tight end, Chuck Romano, became a baby daddy for the fourth time and with a fourth woman —a nineteen-year-old cheerleader for the Mercenaries.

That whole situation was a nightmare for the press office.

Managing their reputation will be a doozy, so it's smart the team is battening down the hatches on that regard. Ever since they foolishly traded away Beck Cafferty to lead the San Francisco Renegades, the Mercenaries have been a pothole of problems.

But the GM—KP Loraine—has zero patience for shenanigans of any sort. In the last few months, she's let go of the defensive back and the nose guard. She dumped Romano from the roster too, when his contract came due at the end of the season. Probably not the toughest decision since he was coming off a terrible year on the field.

Still, she cleaned house with a no-bullshit broom, and then made some sharp trades, like nabbing wide receiver Gabe Clements. He's an NFL veteran, and won a SuperBowl. Plus, in college, Gabe played with Sanders, the Mercenaries QB, so those two guys should be a solid pair leading the team in the huddle.

I'm nearly finished reading articles and scouting reports that afternoon when Stephen raps on the door and strides into my office.

"So...something came up," he says in that unreadable voice. "With the whole...player thing."

Well, that could be anything.

Could be something about the *situation* he mentioned, could be news that the new receiver is leading a cock-fighting ring.

I brace myself but put on an *I can handle anything* face. "What's the news, boss? I'll handle it."

He sighs. "This one." He shakes his head. "Man..."

Spit it out.

"It's Sanders," he continues.

My stomach drops. Dear God, I hope he didn't become the next player to land in hot water. "What happened with him?"

Stephen mimes slicing a knife over his own shoulder. "Labral tear in the shoulder. Needs surgery. Out of commission for twelve weeks."

"Ouch," I say, wincing in sympathy for the pain Sanders must be going through. "That's terrible. What's next? The backup is decent enough."

"He is, but the GM made a trade a few days ago. Looks like Loraine just wrapped it up this afternoon, so we wanted you to take a look at the two press releases before we head to the event. The new player should be making his debut there."

"Sounds good. I'll get on it now," I reply. Because there's clearly no time to lose.

"Great. I just emailed you the statements. Back in ten?"

"Of course," I swivel my chair toward the

computer and toggle over to my inbox. This should be an easy-in, easy-out scenario. I seriously doubt the injury statement will require any lawyering, but when you need to fix a bad rep, you can't cut corners, even on something as simple as a statement about a quarterback requiring surgery.

Carefully, I read it all. Everything looks good, but one line needs a minor tweak. I make an edit, then flip to the next release.

The first paragraph makes me blink.

The words rise up from the page, beating like they're alive.

The Mercenaries are thrilled to share that they've traded for Drew Adams from the Los Angeles Devil Sharks. The quarterback, who has a top-ten passer rating, will be moving across town to the Mercenaries and will likely start in the first game of the season.

7

SPANK ME WITH A TACO

Drew

When Maddox hit me with the news, it wasn't the trade that surprised me. My old team had been releasing players left and right during the off-season to reduce payroll. I figured my number would be up soon, and they'd bounce me to Baltimore, Miami, or maybe Seattle. Someplace with a weakness behind the center.

But a trade where I don't even have to pack up my things?

That was a helluva surprise, and some Midas-touch level agenting from Maddox.

Maybe some of Carter's football luck is rubbing off on me. The Mercenaries aren't a bad team. They've just been toxic off the field, and that shit has a way of following you into games and messing with your head.

With the deal finally done, I embrace the change with open arms, and on Thursday, I head to the Mercenaries practice field.

It's a tough one, but a damn good one. By the time practice ends, my muscles are drained and I'm sweat-soaked, but I can't complain. This is how practice should be.

I walk off the field with Gabe Clements, the team's new receiver who's known around the league for his smooth hands, his predatory intensity on the field, and his unwavering devotion to pre-game rituals.

He claps me on the back. "Nice work, Adams. And thanks for taking my spot as the new guy. It's been hell with them calling me The New Dude all throughout training camp, but it looks like you just got that nickname."

"Happy to take it on."

"Excellent, New Dude. Now, let's show the whole city why they traded for us this year."

That's what I want—a receiver corps that's focused on the game of football. I offer a fist for knocking. "Let's do it."

He knocks back. "We're gonna blast out of the tunnel for the first game like we're fucking cheetahs," he says. "Cheetahs with hacky sacks."

Hometown trades aside, I'm not usually

surprised. But...hacky sacks? "Google translate please," I say.

"New Dude, I'm with a new team. I need a new ritual. I retired my yoyo from last season. I was a hacky sack ace in college."

"Along with a Rose Bowl-winning receiver?"

He arches a brow, clearly impressed with my knowledge. "Multi-talented is my middle name. Anyway, I'm switching to hacky sacks for my new pre-game ritual. You in?"

I'm not a ritual guy, but if Gabe is, then I'll go along with it. "I'm in." I take a beat as we reach the tunnel. "But maybe send me a calendar item so I don't forget?"

He growls. "You won't forget, New Dude."

"You're right. I won't. Seriously, you can count me in. You, me, we're a package deal."

Gabe cracks a small smile. "Yes, we are," he says, squaring his shoulders and walking a little taller.

Good. I want him to know I'll have his back, and I hope he'll have mine. That's how we'll need to work together on the field—with trust and support.

"I'll throw 'em as long as you catch 'em," I say.

He holds his arms out wide. "We'll get along just fine then, New Dude. Because these arms were made to cradle the ball."

I like Gabe's brand of cocky confidence.

We head indoors, the blast of cool air-conditioning a welcome relief from the heat. I glance around the concrete hallway, still getting used to the look and feel of the facilities.

But I sure like getting used to it.

The Mercenaries aren't perfect by any stretch. This team has plenty of problems. But it's spending on players rather than cutting them.

That means we have a real chance to win. Especially if I have anything to say about it.

And I do.

* * *

After I shower and dress, I take one last look in the mirror. Sharp vest, fine shirt, smooth shave. I look like an athlete who cleans up well.

Just what Maddox said the team wanted from me when we talked at the café the other day. "You have the stats, the track record, and you're in the last year of a contract they're willing to pick up. Plus, you don't cause trouble off the field," he'd said.

"I'm so innocent," I'd joked.

With a wink, Maddox patted my shoulder and said, "Only your agent and your priest know the truth."

And Carter had quipped, "And I already heard his confession."

The team had one other stipulation—no more paddle boarding, surfing or other water sports. Most are low-risk sports, they acknowledged. But they don't let their players paddle board in the waves. That was a choice the Devil Sharks made. I get that, but I also got the subtext—the Devil Sharks were lazy. They didn't care. And—no surprise—they didn't win. The Mercenaries are changing their tune and caring about *everything.*

I'm just glad paddle boarding was allowed on the weekend that I got hit in the head.

I leave the locker room, looking for Stephen. The team's EVP said he'd meet me here to give me the deets on the event he wants me to attend. I find him quickly—he's got a Humphrey Bogart cool to him with slicked back gray hair and a chiseled jaw.

He stands across the hall, his head bent over his phone. When the door shuts with a snick, he lifts his face, slides his phone in his pocket, and strides up to me.

"Hey, Drew," he says, parking a hand on my shoulder. His eyes match his hair—they're almost silvery. "All set for the youth sports fundraiser tonight?"

"Absolutely," I say. "It's a cause near and dear."

"Great. Really appreciate you doing this so last minute. Almost as much as I appreciate you being on our team."

"I'm psyched for the chance," I say. "I've been wanting to do some work with a local charity that supports underprivileged youth sports."

"Great. Lots of folks from the organization will be

there, so I'll make sure you meet everyone and that they all know our new quarterback," he says with a quick smile. "And you'll smile for the cameras. Get some Instagram posts, make a few comments to the sports sites. You know the drill. I'll introduce you to the press department and some of the front office people you'll be working with."

"Can't wait," I say. This is what I want in a team. A front office that gets behind its players. That supports them. That works with the community.

"I have to take care of a few things here. But I'll meet you in the lobby of the hotel. I texted you the address."

"I'll be there."

The fact that the EVP himself is looking out for me tells me all I need to know about the Mercenaries —they're ready to take a chance this season at going the distance.

This is my chance too, and I plan to make the most of being a Mercenary in every single way.

I also plan to have some good, clean fun tonight after the event. There's nothing wrong with seeing a woman who saved me from a deadly paddle board oar. Hell, that's a good-guy story right there. And when we're done with tacos and ice cream, we'll go to her place, close the door, and leave the world behind.

Yup. My luck in football and romance is turning around.

* * *

I catch up on messages in the back of the Lyft on the way to the event. First, I click on a text from my buddy Milo in New York. The fucker sent me a link to a new dating column his girlfriend writes—The Virgin Club Alum, and the article is titled *Top Five Signs You're Doing It Wrong.*

I groan, but hats off to him.

Milo: I've learned so much about women from this column, but maybe you need to read it more religiously. I mean, just a thought from the headline. Does seem up your alley.

Ha. Like he can pull a fast one on me. I'm the guy who figured out who his new lady was well before he did.

Drew: Bookmarking this to read tonight AFTER my smoking-hot date. Wait. Make that…a tomorrow read.

Then I toggle to Carter's text.

Carter: Dude. Did you see this new barber shop nearby? They do shaves beachside! I'm flying to town tonight and doing this tomorrow.

Drew: Do you not know how to work a razor yourself? I can set you up with some lessons with a thirteen-year-old who's offering them to helpless dudes.

Carter: Have you ever had a real shave? By a pro? You will NOT go back to doing it yourself. It's like sex in self-care form.

Drew: That would be rubbing one out, buddy. It already exists.

Carter: You don't deserve the grooming equivalent of ejaculation.

Drew: I bet the barber is just dying to have you schedule an appointment now.

Carter: Already scheduled one in your name. Thanks, man.

My friends are such dicks. Fucking love them.

Then, I shift gears into good-boy mode as I click on today's text from my mom. She sends me the *Daily Double*, as she calls it. A pic of the latest antics from my twin sisters.

Mom: Today, Mira and Sophie turned into identical mermaids. Can you tell them apart?

The little sea creatures are wearing fake fishtails with their bathing suits and splashing around in the pool, red hair whipping everywhere. Good-boy mode is so easy to engage with those two cuties and my awesome mom. I reply with my best guess, but I suspect they'll be tricking everyone, especially their parents, for a long time. They are as identical as twins come.

I send Mom another note.

Drew: You doing okay? Or are you exhausted? Let me know if you need anything.

Mom: I've been exhausted for twenty-eight years, but I wouldn't change a thing.

My heart squeezes with affection. But at least she's not working herself to the bone like she was when she was a single mom, raising a kid alone. She handled it all, working late nights, but showing up for every game. My senior year of high school, she met a good dude on the apps, falling hard for a mechanical engineer who dotes on her and their two girls—their *oops and we don't regret it* babies.

After what my dad put her through, leaving her with nothing, she deserves the love and affection she gets from her husband.

She also deserves this pool that she's lounging by at her home in Sherman Oaks.

The pool came from me. Bought it last year for her as a long overdue gift, since she always used to joke that someday she'd lounge by the pool.

Drew: Glad you and the doubles are enjoying the water. I'll come see you soon, but you'd better bring those mermaids to my first game!

Mom: Trident himself couldn't keep them away. They love rooting for their big brother.

I close the thread with Mom as the car slows at a light. I check the time, figuring I should be at the hotel in fifteen minutes. Even though the event should be fun, I'm counting down the seconds till *after* the meet and greet when I get to see Brooke again. I'm stoked to tell her about the trade and then talk about anything besides football.

Maybe I'll mention the trade to her in a text, so we won't have to talk shop over tacos. I'd rather talk sex positions and what makes her tick. My goal tonight? Getting to know her better.

Then, getting to know her better in bed.

Oh, shit.

I haven't told her I'll be late.

I return to my text app, then fire off a new note to her.

Drew: Hey, rock star goddess surf angel. I have to do a work thing this evening, but I should be able to meet you at eight at Tacos Are Life. But I promise the delay will be worth it. I'll owe you an extra O for my tardiness.

Then, as I wait for her reply, I read our prior notes.

There's the one from Sunday when we made

plans while we were in her kitchen. Plus, the text I sent this morning.

Drew: Tacos. I can't stop thinking about tacos.

Her reply was pure Brooke.

IOU: I never stop thinking about tacos.

She even wrote back again this afternoon, adding, *Can't wait to devour tacos—and you.*

Rawr. The woman does like dirty talk. I replied with *If I weren't heading into practice right now, I would tell you all the ways I want to devour you.*

Tell me later, big stud, she'd said.

There's time before we reach the hotel in Santa Monica to give her some more of my ideas. While the driver navigates through traffic, I tap out another text.

But before I hit send, my phone rings with a call from my buddy Patrick, and I answer right away. Bet he has good money news. "Let me guess. You made money turn into more money today."

He laughs, then says, "So much you're going to build a shrine to me for what I did."

"Is that so?"

"It's going to be one hundred feet tall, and you will lay gifts at my feet."

"Are you dead in this scenario? Are you lying in the shrine? Paint the picture more fully for me. Don't leave out a single detail."

"And maybe I won't tell you about the sweet deal I just got on a new IPO. *For you*."

"Tell me. You know you want to," I goad.

My longtime friend rattles off details of a stock trade he made for me when a new app went public this morning. It's all Martian to me, but Patrick is a finance wizard, which is why he handles my portfolio. We go way back, and he's magic when it comes to ROI.

"That sounds a lot like blah, blah, blah to my ears, but your blah, blah, blah usually makes me dollar signs, so go forth and do it," I say.

"I am the king of blah, blah, blah," he says, then takes a beat, shifting gears. "You ready for tonight? You feeling good? Need anything?"

Patrick is the big brother I never had. We grew up in the same apartment building, and our moms were best friends too. Still are. He's two years older so he likes to check in on me, and it's kind of sweet.

"I am. It should be fun. I hope the vibe is chill

and not all *tell me about the baby daddies and where they went*."

"And if anyone does ask you about the players who are gone, you just say *I'm just here to play football. Repeat after me.*"

"I'm just here to play football," I echo.

"Bingo. You can indeed be trained."

I arf like a seal.

"Good boy," Patrick says, then we say goodbye and hang up.

I return to my app, eager to keep chatting with my date, especially since—from the looks of the driver's GPS—we've got about one more mile to go.

Plenty of time to pre-game with some dirty texting.

Drew: The countdown is on. In one hour and thirty minutes, I will be feeding you, and then fucking you.

IOU: Oh yeah, you will. But wait. Are you gonna do both at the same time?

Drew: Ha ha. Funny girl. You do love to catch me on technicalities. Let me amend my previous text. I will feed you, then fuck you, and then fuck you again and again till you're shouting my name.

IOU: That all sounds good. But I'm totes down for

feeding *and* fucking too. Can you pull off that feat, stud?

My brow knits. Hmm. Is Brooke into food play? If that's what the lady wants, I'll read up on the best way to bring food into the bedroom. Chocolate sauce maybe? Cherries? Not my thing, but I'm game to try, and the lady has thrown down a challenge.

Drew: Say the word. I'll get chocolate sauce.

IOU: I guess we're still on for the all-you-can-eat buffet tonight.

Drew: I will spend as much time between your sweet legs as I possibly can. But confession: I'd really like to spank you too, and I bet you'd like that.

IOU: Well, I have been a very bad girl.

Drew: Then I will punish you with my palm.

IOU: Ooh, punish me, baby.

I side-eye the device. That's not entirely her style. *Baby*? But then again, she's amping up the dirty talk big time over text.

Trouble is, I'm about to walk into an event sporting wood.

Drew: All right, honey, I need to concentrate on being a good guy for the next hour before I see you and take care of all your bedroom needs.

IOU: Bet you'll be thinking of spanking me with a taco.

I blink in confusion. What the hell has got into Brooke tonight? No idea, but it's time to put her out of my mind since we've reached the hotel. I didn't even mention the trade, but there's time for that later.

I say goodbye to the driver, then step out of the car, and walk toward the art deco hotel with the peach pastel façade. The sun dips low in the lavender sky over the ocean, and I snap a quick pic to send to Mom. *Next time you get a sitter, I'll put you and Tom up here. This place looks sweet!*

Tucking my phone away, I head inside, spotting Stephen in a corner of the lobby, talking into his phone. Once he sees me, he puts the device away. He escorts me to the ballroom, all exposed pipes and concrete walls, then introduces me to several people with the youth sports organization. A photographer snaps shots the whole time, and I play the role that's hardly a role—the outgoing, non-troublemaking, peace-loving quarterback, who doesn't throw punches or raise hell.

After I chat with some of the biggest donors, Stephen shepherds me to an olive-skinned, bearded man who, it turns out, heads up this charity.

"Drew, I want you to meet Paul Tavarez with Young Athletes. Paul, this is Drew Adams. He joined our team today as the quarterback. We're thrilled to have him on board, especially since he's already active with many wonderful charitable endeavors," Stephen says to the bearded man.

"Nice to meet you, Paul. Love the work you're doing to create opportunities for kids who need and want it. I was one of those kids once upon a time," I say, shaking Paul's hand. "And I'd love to get more involved."

"Music to my ears," Paul says, beaming.

We talk for a few minutes about how I'd like to get more involved when Stephen drops a hand on my shoulder.

"There's someone else I want you to meet," he says, then guides me away from Paul and toward a high table in the corner. "My right-hand woman is sharp as a tack. She makes sure we don't fumble," he says, then winks in case I didn't realize he was making a joke.

I smile to let him know I get it—fumbling humor and all. Then my smile widens when my gaze narrows in on...

That's my rock star goddess surf angel.

And she's even sexier than she was on Sunday. Brooke is hot as sin in a red skirt, white blouse, and black heels, her blonde hair flowing over her shoulders. The businesswoman look is almost enough to make me forget my name—

Wait. Hold the fuck on.

What is Brooke doing here?

Oh, I bet I know. Her baseball team's probably involved with the charity too.

That must be it. Luck is on my side in all the things—romance, football, traffic.

Yay me.

Stephen leads me her way, and I try to rein in a grin, the whole time thinking about kissing Brooke, touching her, stripping her naked later tonight.

But when I reach her and her eyes lock with mine, Brooke almost seems like a different person. Her genuine smile from the beach is gone, replaced by a plastic grin. Her warm brown eyes are cold.

What's that all about?

"Drew, this is Brooke Holland. She's my top attorney. She's been working for the Bandits, and the

Carlisles just added the football team to her responsibilities, which means she handles legal work for
the Mercenaries, too," he says.

And it turns out I'm now working with the
woman who wants me to spank her with tacos
tonight.

8

NAUGHTY LITTLE GOBLINS

Brooke

I've never been one to run away from a challenge, but now seems like a good time to slap on some sneakers and start.

I've had two hours since Stephen dropped the news on me this afternoon about Drew coming to the Mercenaries. Two hours to figure out how to act when seeing my Sunday night hookup, but I'm no closer to an answer than I was when I left the office. After dropping my car at home so I could change my clothes, I caught a Lyft here. I've spent the last hour at this event chatting with donors and executives, and basically avoiding Drew.

Yet I can't avoid him any longer. He's heading my way with Stephen.

This is weirder than when we were in bed and I didn't know what to do with my hands.

What do I do with my whole body now? Do I lean casually against the bar? Maybe flick some hair off my shoulder? Wait. I'll take a drink.

I knock back a gulp of my water. Then I flip mentally through my group text with Cara and my good friend Rachel. On the way over, I begged them for advice on how to handle seeing the hookup who ghosted me who's now become the hotly anticipated new player on the team I work for.

Cara's advice? *Be cool. Be badass. Be yourself.*

Rachel's words of wisdom? *He doesn't deserve you. Mark my words—he's going to be trotting after you tonight, begging for text forgiveness. Have no mercy. Not one ounce. You are badass.*

Right now, I don't feel badass. I feel foolish because Drew's in front of me, offering me a hand and smiling curiously. "Nice to meet you, Brooke," he says, upbeat.

So that's how we do it? We pretend we don't know each other?

Oh, right. Of course we do. I can't tell Stephen I screwed our new quarterback and then he blew me off.

My stomach roils.

This is such a disaster. I would rather be interviewed by The Shirtless Esquire than talk to Drew. At least I have a buffer, though, in Stephen.

I extend my free hand. "Pleasure to meet you Drew. We're excited you'll be leading the team," I say.

There. I'm such a pro.

"Me too." Drew's lips twitch. Seeing me again must be the height of amusement for him. The asshole. It's not funny that he ditched me. It hurt, and I didn't like being misled.

"I heard about your trade this afternoon, right after Stephen told me about my promotion." I coolly drop in that pertinent info. Drew might be a dick, but I don't want him to think I am. I definitely don't want him to think I lied about my job. There's only one liar among us.

Except, did I just sound like I'm tooting my own horn?

Yeah, I did.

Groan.

Drew meets my gaze, his focus solely on me. "Good for you on the promotion. That must be—"

He cuts himself off before he says anything more. Anything like *I knew you were down on your job the day I met you and led you on. Sure, I never replied, but good for you in moving up, lady-boss style.*

At least, he has enough sense to fake things.

"I'm excited for the new opportunity," I say.

Stephen flashes a rare smile. "So am I. The hardest part was not saying a damn word when you didn't get the promotion. But I had bigger things planned for you." He clears his throat, his gaze drifting briefly around the room, like he's scanning for something. "Ah. I need to chat with Paul for a few. Drew, if you need anything, Brooke is the legal liaison to the press department this season. She's tasked with helping to make sure we present the best public face, and don't break any rules. I'll let you two get to know each other since I need to chat with a few folks."

Then he spins on his heel and takes off.

I gulp. My buffer is gone. I am all alone with the man I desperately wanted to see again but who didn't want to see me.

I take another drink of my water. And that was a rookie mistake. My skull turns to tundra. I fight off a wince. I will not let Drew see my face contort from the brain freeze. I ignore the ice headache as I say, "What a great event."

What a bland comment.

But I can barely think. My forehead is still pulsing with a mind-numbing headache. I grit my teeth.

"You okay?"

"I'm fine," I bite out, then I draw in air and smile wider. The pain starts to ebb.

"You sure?"

"Of course," I say, "Congratulations on joining the team. Everyone is thrilled to have you."

He smirks again. "You said that already."

My face flushes. Great. Now he's pointing out my mistakes. Real fun.

I can't be around him right now. I need a moment to regroup. "Excuse me, Drew," I say, and I jet off, leaving the ballroom and rushing to the ladies' room, my brain freeze melting off along the way.

Once inside, I grab my phone and dial Rachel's number. She owns a jewelry boutique on the main drag in Venice and the store probably just closed.

Thankfully, my friend answers right away, and I dive into my emergency. "He's here, like I suspected he'd be, and I'm doing such a bang-up job at being a badass that I ran into the ladies' room to hide." I spin around, hunting for an escape hatch. "Can I just pull down the air vent like they do in the movies and crawl out?"

"That's an option. Maybe not a wise one, but it's one nonetheless."

I gaze upward at the vent, doing some quick calculations. "It's seven feet high. Maybe I can step on the sink and sort of swing my legs up."

"Sure. That doesn't sound likely to break your neck at all."

I assess the distance. "I think I can make it."

"Or just a wild idea. You could face him. And be merciless, like I said."

Closing my eyes, I slump against the sink. "The worst part is he's all...*cheery*."

"Bastard," she mutters. "That pisses me off."

Then she seems to brighten, or perhaps turn devil-ishly clever since she says, "Oh, wait. If he's acting like he didn't ditch you, you should do the same to him."

I perk up. Lift my face. "I should?"

"Yes, pretend you never texted him. Act like you're cool with everything. Don't let on you were checking your phone like it was going to give birth."

That's genius, birthing analogy aside. "You're brilliant and I love you," I say, then hang up.

When I turn around, I take a deep breath, smooth my hands down my skirt, then leave, ready to resume normal human operations again.

But when I exit the restroom, I stifle a shriek.

The tall, broad, and too-handsome quarterback waits here in the hall, away from the event and the crowds. His hazel eyes brim with concern. "Hey," he says gently. "Are you okay?"

Pretend, Brooke.

I lift my chin defiantly. My queen move. Then I smile for the camera. "I'm fabulous. Just had to powder my nose," I say, waving my clutch toward the restroom.

He arches an eyebrow. Even that simple gesture is impossibly sexy on him. But then, he has an unfair advantage because he's decked out in tailored pants, a dress shirt, and a vest that fits him like a glove. If he wasn't already stunning, the damn vest alone would send him to the top of the hot list.

I've seen him in shorts, and now I've seen him in a suit. The man makes the clothes every time.

The universe is a joker.

"I had no idea you were going to be here," he says, in a thoughtful tone—that tone makes zero sense. "But the job sounds good?"

Why is he being so nice? "Yes. Like I said, I just found out today. They added football to my purview. So I guess we're working together," I say with the biggest grin I can muster.

No way am I letting on how hurt I was by his silent treatment. I don't want to get wounded again. I still have scars from Sailor's trickery.

I angle my body toward the ballroom, hoping Drew gets the message that it's time to return to the event.

"I was shocked too," Drew adds, still chatting in spite of my best efforts to grow wings. "I was going to tell you about the trade when we texted earlier," he says as I take a step down the hall.

What did he just say?

I stop and turn back to him, lifting a brow. "Excuse me?"

He smiles, flirty and just a touch embarrassed— but sexy embarrassed—as he glances around and lowers his voice. "You know. About the tacos, and the chocolate sauce, and the yada yada yada."

I know nothing about this yada.

I frown. "What texts, Drew?"

He steps closer, leans into me, his mouth dangerously near to my ear. I shiver. Stupid body. "You know—when you let on you're into food play," Drew whispers, his voice low and husky and turning me on even though I'm not into food play.

I am, however, into solving problems.

I step back, meet his eyes. "We didn't text, so I'm not sure what you mean. I haven't heard from you since you left my house." And I will prove it, stat. Reaching into my clutch, I grab my phone, unlock it, and click to my texts. "See?" I say, eager to show him the evidence.

He peers at my screen, studying the messages from Sunday, then my text to him on Monday about changing the time for tonight. There's no reply from him. The chain ends there.

Such a sad text thread.

So empty.

"Oh, shit," he mutters, then drags a hand down his face in slow, motion. "I should have known you'd never call me *stud* or *baby*." He sounds mortified.

He pulls his phone from his pocket. "I never got your message on Monday about the time. But I *thought* we were texting," he says, sheepishly. "Because of this..."

He shows me the screen he's pulled up, and I read a slew of messages between Drew and IOU. My eyes widen, flicking from the screen to him as I follow this bawdy thread.

By the end, I can barely contain my laughter. "Drew, I think you have two IOUs," I whisper through my chuckles.

"Ya think?" he asks drily. "I just want to know which of my jackass friends pulled this off."

"Someone who's going to be crowing about it for a long time," I say with admiration for the architect of this joke. Someone worked him over big time. "But how did this happen?"

Before he can attempt to answer, his phone beeps. The name IOU appears in the notification window but there's a picture of a dark-haired man smirking, next to the words *Did you spank her with tacos yet?*

Drew groans. In guy language, that loosely translates to *I can't believe that fucker tricked me.* He shakes his head. "I have to tip my cap to my buddy."

"But what happened? You wrote back to me on Sunday night and I got it. And then nothing?"

His brow knits, cogs turning as he thinks. Then the circuit closes and he winces at what he's about to say. "This is going to sound incredibly ridic, but I had to reset my phone on Monday morning because it was doing wonky phone shit. I don't know if it was the sand on Sunday or it was possessed by goblins or what."

Naughty little goblins seem like a far-fetched dating excuse, but he showed me the text thread. I'll at least let him tell me the rest of the story. "And what did the goblins do?"

"They fucked shit up!" he says with a laugh. At least he can handle being the butt of a joke. "The update could have merged my contacts and made Patrick's number the default IOU. Your message on Monday could have been filtered." He clicks on his screen again and curses. "Fuck."

He shows me the phone and there's my note, no contact name attached, filtered into "unknown callers." If he's making this up, he went to a lot of trouble to fake the proof.

"So does this also mean if you know ten Davids they're now one David?"

He looks horrified at the idea. "I better check on that. My friend David runs a sweet new tapas place, but this other David from high school tries to sell me Muscle Milk all the time. I'd hate to mix them up."

"Understandable. But how do you have another IOU in your contacts?"

Drew drags a hand through his hair, maybe a little chagrined. When he meets my gaze, his vulnerable expression tugs on my heart. I don't want to sound like I'm doubting him if this is a tough topic.

In his silence, I add gently, "I'm just curious. But you don't have to tell me. Truly, it's fine."

"I don't mind," he says quietly, but it sounds like he's gearing up to reveal something personal. "I didn't have a lot of money growing up. My buddy

Patrick didn't either, but when we got to college, he started figuring out the stock market and started making money. I was still scraping by, so he'd help me out from time to time. I named him IOU as a joke between us. He didn't mind, but it always embarrassed me a little that I had to ask."

I'm touched that he'd share that. "Sounds like he's a good friend. I'm glad you had him to turn to."

"He's a good guy. He's my financial advisor now, which works out well for both of us." He blows out a long breath, letting his embarrassment go. Good humor comes in its place, his eyes twinkling. "Somehow, I completely missed that he was pulling a fast one."

I laugh at the absurdity of the whole situation, from the prank to his friend seizing the moment.

I'm ready to let him off the hook except for one thing. I arch a brow, quoting Patrick's impersonation of me. "*That all sounds good. But I'm totes down for feeding and fucking too. Can you pull off that feat, stud?*" I stare at Drew, a smile on my face. "That wasn't the tip-off you weren't texting me?"

He shrugs sheepishly. "It didn't entirely sound like you—the stud part especially. But I didn't want to be judge-y about how you talked over text."

I lift the other brow. "*Punish me, baby?*"

He tosses up his hands. "Maybe you liked bondage and stuff."

"*I've been a bad girl?*"

He holds up his hands in surrender. "Hey, now. No judgies."

"None from me," I say, enjoying the same rapport as we did on Sunday. "But that's not what I'd say."

Drew parks his hands on his hips, issuing me a challenging stare. "What would *you* say, Surf Angel?"

I step closer, part my lips, lick them, and say, "Smack my ass. Hard. Harder. Yes. Just like that."

His breath comes out staggered. "Brooke," he says in a warning.

I do need to stop flirting, for real. When we slept together on Sunday, we weren't working together. But now we are. I've stepped into a new job, the team is on reputation rehab, and Drew has a chance to show what he's made of professionally.

I hate to say this. Truly I do. But there is no other choice. "We can't go out tonight. Or at all."

He's quiet at first, impassive. I can picture him watching a game from the sidelines, giving nothing away. Then, with disappointment, he nods. "I had a feeling."

"With the trouble the team has been through, we can't take a chance of anything that would be..." I pause, hunting for the word. "Inappropriate. Even remotely inappropriate."

No way in hell would management want a lawyer diddling with a player.

"Of course. We don't want to put the team in a bad light," he says. It's a relief that he understands the full scope of the disaster another night together could be.

"And it's your first year here," I add. "We both have a lot at stake."

"Exactly. Gotta keep everything above board." Drew's mood shifts from disappointed to playful. "But I bet there's no rule that we can't be friends. How's that for a technicality?"

I can't help it. I smile too. This man could charm the panties off me any day.

I mean, the pants.

He's totally not charming my thong off. That little lacy number is staying where it belongs.

"That's a good technicality. Let's be friends," I say, and we shake on it.

My one-night stand is now officially off-limits in the bedroom.

As friends, we return to the ballroom and join my colleagues and the people from the charity. We chat and nibble on appetizers, Drew posing for photos in front of the banner.

He's the opposite of the guys from last year.

There's no scowl to be seen for miles.

He's so photogenic. That smile that dazzled me the day I met him on the beach is shining at full wattage. My chest warms as I look at him.

Someone nudges me and I startle, then relax when I realize it's Stephen. "It's like hiring America's guy next door for the quarterback," my boss says at a low volume, shaking his head in admiration.

"That's a pretty apt description," I agree.

"He's going to make our lives so much easier if this keeps up. The camera loves him," he says. "When you add in the mom, the kid sisters, the life-long friends—it's a PR dream."

He might as well blow a chef's kiss. Stephen's got a vision for his new golden guy. He'll serve it up to the media, and the media will love it.

"That would make our lives easier," I say.

He grins, diabolically pleased. Then he tips his chin toward the guy with the magic arm and the perfect rep. "Let's grab a photo of you with him too."

I shoot him the side-eye.

"No. Seriously. I want pictures of him every-where. I want to show the world we're a united team, from management to the players, here at the Mercenaries."

I slap on my poker face and slide in next to the star.

"Lucky me," Drew whispers.

But we're sort of unlucky too.

When the event winds down, Paul from the charity corrals Drew into a long conversation, and it's time for me to call it a night. I say goodbye to Stephen, thanking him again for the horchata and the promotion, then I head to the lobby to call a Lyft.

I enter my location in the app, but before I can finish, I hear footsteps.

I stop tapping. I turn around. Drew's by my side.

"You're not leaving without saying goodbye, are you?"

"Of course not. Just ordering a Lyft. I was going to say goodbye."

He covers my hand with his. "Don't take a Lyft. Let's walk for a bit. As friends."

So, as friends, we leave together.

9

MY HARDSHIP

Drew

I don't want a consolation prize with Brooke, but I also don't want to go home yet. So in this case, I take the consolation prize. I hold the door for her as we go, glancing toward the ocean, the waves crashing nearby.

"Have you been paddle boarding since that fateful day?" she asks.

"No. And I won't be paddle boarding again," I say, explaining that the Mercenaries GM added it to the list of forbidden activities. "I'm just glad paddle boarding was allowed when I got hit on the head with that guy's oar."

She smiles. "Me too."

I gesture to the sidewalk. "But walking? I'm allowed to walk as much as I want."

"Walking makes us outliers. No one walks in Los Angeles," she remarks as we stop at Colorado Avenue.

"Or we're caught in a time warp," I suggest helpfully.

She plays along. "Maybe even a parallel universe."

"Maybe one where you don't work for my team." I shoot her a flirty smile and I have no regrets.

"Oh, I definitely don't work with you in that world," she says, returning my grin as we cross the street.

In the real world, we run the risk of being a scandal. If word got out somehow that I was administering orgasms to a team executive, I'd look like a playboy. Perception is everything there.

But in this alternate world, we're just a baller and a lawyer heading down the street, through the throngs of people in Santa Monica, I toss out another question. "But aren't they walking too, in Los Angeles? Are they in the parallel universe?"

"Hmm. Technically they are walking, but I feel like they're walking in exploration. We're walking as a form of commuting and no one does that, so we remain in our parallel universe."

"You are the queen of technicalities," I say.

She mimes adjusting a tiara, then gestures to the nearby pier. "And in our parallel lives, we're going to the pier. Which is home to one of my favorite activities."

"Besides reading and losing your mind over my dirty talk?" I ask, and oops. Went there again. Oh well.

She rolls her eyes but nudges my elbow. "Yes, Drew. Besides those two. My third favorite hobby is playing Whac-A-Mole."

"Who's dirty talking now, Brooke?"

"Whac-A-Mole is like a sushi hand roll. They can't not sound naughty."

"Maybe both are," I say, then pat my stomach. "And now I want to take you out for sushi."

"Mmm. Sushi sounds great," she says. "In our time warp, of course."

I groan, missing both sushi and our date. "You're tempting me, woman."

"Sushi and Whac-A-Mole are your weaknesses too?"

"Yes. Hell yes." And I can't resist a little more flirting so in a low, smoky voice, I add, "Among other things."

She takes a shaky breath and seems to recenter herself, tucking a strand of hair behind her ear. "What else would we be doing on the pier? Whac-A-Mole and sushi and...?"

Easy answer. "Skee-Ball. That's one of my favorite things to do. When I went to New York earlier in the summer to visit my cousin, I schooled him and his friends in Skee-Ball." I bump my shoulder to hers, maybe because I'm taking what I can get. "I'm fucking awesome at Skee-Ball."

"I should hope so, with that magic arm of yours," she says with her trademark sass.

I wiggle my fingers. "I have good hands too."

She shakes her head, amused. "Why do I feel like you can turn anything into a naughty comment?"

"Because I can. Except I shouldn't," I say, resigning myself to our reality. "Especially since I got fooled by naughty comments this afternoon."

"Please tell Patrick he wins the award for best prankster. His prank was so good, I almost don't even care that I was so bummed you didn't text."

I hate that she thought I was ditching her. "I was so not ghosting you."

She frowns. "I know that now. But you should have seen the curses my friends and I lobbed at you."

I bring my hand to my heart, defending past me. "Here I was being a good guy, sending you texts, checking in, and you thought I was a world-class jackass," I say.

She winces but nods. "The whole time before the event, I was racking my brain to figure out how to handle seeing this guy who had left me in the dust," she says as we pass a sidewalk café with a view of the water. For a few seconds, I wish we could duck in there, grab some drinks, nosh on appetizers.

That thought is a little detour from our conversation. "Meanwhile, I *was* thinking about tonight. How I was going to tell you the trade news over text, so we didn't get bogged down with work bullshit over dinner."

She looks at me with delight. "You had a whole plan for just talking to me?"

"Oh yeah," I say, telling her what I'd considered. "At dinner, I planned to focus on getting to know you."

I still want that. She's a fascinating mix of smart and funny, awkward and sassy. She's not afraid to bust my chops, and I enjoy the hell out of her company.

"Aww," Brooke says, sounding legitimately touched. "That's sweet." She shoots me an apologetic look. "And I feel terrible now."

I wish she didn't think I was a schmuck for the last few days, so I want to seal the deal on the rep of past me. "No need to feel bad, especially since you're now aware what an awesome date I'd have been," I say with a grin.

"And you are, it seems, since this is kind of like a great second date. In our parallel universe. And I'm curious. What did you want to get to know about me?"

"Anything," I say, emphatically. "What makes you tick. You said you have a sister. What's she like?"

That's an easy start.

Brooke lights up as she tells me about Cara, her bright outlook on life, how hard she studies, her drive to be a special education teacher. "I'm proud of her, especially since she's almost debt free. I didn't want her to be like me, weighed down with loans."

I grimace. "That's got to be an inevitability of law school," I say with sympathy.

"It is, but hey, no one feels bad for lawyers. And in a couple years, I'll have them paid off. But that's another reason I was in a funk about work when I met you. I thought I'd been passed over. But then it turned out I got a new job and a raise."

I grin and offer a hand to high-five. She smacks back. This is not the way I want to congratulate her on her promotion. A hot kiss would be better. "That is awesome," I say, focusing on the positive.

"The flip side is no third date," she says, sounding a little forlorn.

Womp. Womp.

"For the record, I would have asked you on a third date. And I would also have not ghosted you."

"Good to know," she says.

We're quiet for a bit as we walk into the night, my gaze drifting to her shoes. Sexy red skirt that revs my engine. Those black heels. That tight little waist. "By the way, those shoes? I would have had you leave them on tonight," I say, in a voice just for her.

A smile sneaks across her face, deliciously dirty. "Would you have?"

"Absolutely. You naked in those heels? Mmm," I say, enjoying the images my brain is supplying. "I'd put them on my shoulders, around my waist, up in the air."

She lets out a sexy whimper. "You're making this hard."

"Oh, it's definitely hard," I say.

"*Your hardship*," she says, playfully.

"That describes me when I'm with you," I say.

She shoots me a knowing look that says she's onto my dirty thoughts. And she knows the risks of them, since she clears her throat, tsks me, then says, "You mentioned when I met you that you had twin sisters. What are they like?" I suppose it's good that one of us has the self-control to course correct.

Plus, I'm always eager to share deets on the doubles. "They're troublemakers and they trick my mom and her hubs all the time," I say, then grab my phone and show her the mermaid pic.

"They are adorable," she says, then studies my face for a few seconds, like she's making sure she has clearance. "You said they were half-sisters..."

An invitation, giving me the chance to fill in the gaps. So far, I like sharing with Brooke. "My dad took off when I was five, then he died when I was twelve —hard-partying lifestyle, drinking too much, driving too fast."

She squeezes my arm. "That's hard."

"It is but I can't even say I miss him because I

never knew him. All I knew was how he left Mom—
with all the responsibility."

"She raised a damn fine son," Brooke says.

Mom deserves the credit. "She's a good woman. I
have the utmost respect for her. I want to do right by
her. She'll be at my first game."

"I bet you'll love seeing her there."

"And you?" My question is open-ended too, for
the same reasons. She can tell me about her family if
she wants to or not.

"Mom and Dad are still together. He's a high
school football coach. Cara and I try to see them as
often as we can."

"Nice," I say, liking that she has similar priorities
to mine. "Will they come to the game too?"

"Probably. I called to let them know about the
promotion this afternoon. Dad is excited about me
working for a football team now."

"Good man," I say as we pass a billboard for
Sebastian Lowe's new film, a dark superhero flick I
can't wait to see.

"Favorite movie ever," I prompt.

"*Fake Play*, of course," Brooke says, naming a
popular football movie from last decade.

I scoff. "You can't pick a football movie."

"Why not?"

"Because we work in football. Sports movies are
ruled out."

"But it's an awesome movie. And they should not be ruled out."

"Fine. Then let's add *The Time Out* and *Par for the Course*. Also, *Hail Mary*," I add.

"Whoa, reaching way back in the Hall of Fame archives for that one."

"You didn't really think I'd pick *Field of Green*. Everyone picks *Field of Green*."

"Of course I didn't think you'd do that, Drew," she says. "And I do love all of those. The refurbished cinema off Ocean Avenue—Silver Screen Theater—is showing some of the best sports flicks in a few weeks. Including *Fake Play*. You can bet I'll be there."

"No one can resist the pull of *Fake Play*."

"Ha! I knew you loved it after all."

"I never said I didn't," I tease.

"It's the kind of football movie that even non-football fans love."

I scowl. "There are people who don't like football?"

She scoffs dismissively. "I've heard about their existence. Small little pockets on the outskirts of society."

"Seems terribly sad to be such a person."

"It's devastating, Drew," she says, then she roams her eyes over me, like she's cataloguing my face, my chest, my arms, my legs. A soft sigh falls from her lips, a hint of frustration in it. "I'm having such a good time that if I don't catch a Lyft, I'll be tempted."

I love the honesty in her admission. I hate that she's right.

"Me too," I say.

She orders a ride. I wait with her on the corner, hands in my pockets. Then...what the hell. The night is ending. "I wish I were taking you home," I say softly, moving a few inches closer.

"Me too," she says, sounding as wrapped up in longing as I am.

"I want that more now than I did this afternoon," I add.

Her breath hitches. Even though I want to lift my hand, reach for her face, and cup her cheek, I don't.

I'm about to let her go when she meets my gaze, heat flickering in her eyes. "By the way, I would have said yes to spanking."

I groan. She's too sexy. "I would have smacked you exactly the way you wanted it."

"I know."

A fire ignites in my chest, filling me with lust and desire all from those two words. *I know.*

But this kind of talk isn't part of the game plan anymore.

The Nissan we're waiting for arrives, and I reach for the door handle. But before I open it, I grab my phone. Then I enter her number once more—this time under her full name. Brooke Holland, The One and Only. Then I send her a note. ***Had the best time with you tonight.***

She smiles as she reads it, then replies with *Me too.*

I put her in the car and watch her go.

Like a good guy.

10

A VIBE THING

Drew

The sun warms my shoulders. The ocean breeze cools my skin. And the goateed barber slides a sharp blade across my jaw. All the barbers here at Armando's are dressed to the nines in white button-downs, ties, and proper slacks, looking dapper as swing music plays. It's so retro it's cool.

Once I'm done, I'll have to text Brooke a pic. Bet she'd get a kick out of this whole pop-up beachside barber shop here in Venice.

Carter was right. The beachside shave is downright luxurious.

I might start to hum any second.

But I'm *not* going to come. "You getting close, buddy?" I ask Carter in the chair next to mine.

"So close," he grunts like he's holding back his personal satisfaction.

"Behave," I warn.

He laughs a little too big.

"Try to keep still," his barber tells him, a stern fellow with earplugs and a leather apron.

"Like I said, behave," I stage whisper as the owner himself, a goateed guy with steady hands, slides the blade across my jaw one last time then wipes it on a hand towel.

"Smoothest shave ever," he says. "What do you think?"

I pat my cheek. "You're the da Vinci of barbers, my man."

"Thank you. I had lots of practice with my clients in East LA before I opened this shop." Armando tucks the blade into his leather satchel, right next to combs of all sizes, then grabs a tray with lotions and potions. "Pick your scent."

I sit up a little higher and smell the bottles. "This cedar one is nice."

"That's citrus," he says with a chuckle.

"Citrus, cedar. They're both in the C family," I say.

"Close enough," he teases, then pats some aftershave on my face.

When he's done, he holds up a hand mirror, and says with a wicked smile, "Go Mercenaries."

I shake his hand. "Hell yeah." I glance around his busy joint. "And I'll be back."

Carter's done a minute later, so I corral him with our barbers and snap a pic, then post it on social. Stephen should be happy with that. The *only* thing I'm doing wrong is hanging with a rival, so I caption it that way. *Hanging with the enemy, kicking it old school.*

We take off, heading to the main drag in Venice to meet Maddox for lunch. He wanted to catch up on some sponsorship deals for both of us. Carter flew down for his mom's birthday party this weekend, then he'll head back to San Francisco to go into the final week of practice.

"How was your date last night?" Carter asks as we pass a weather-worn bungalow, its shutters beaten from the ocean air over the years.

"It was the best and it was the worst," I say.

"Are you Dickens now?"

"You've heard of Dickens?"

"Yes, asshole. I studied literature in college," Carter says with a scoff.

"And they made you study Dickens?"

"Dude, we were in the same English class."

"I tried to block out memories of Dickens."

He gazes skyward. "Why do I ask you how anything is? Hell, why do I share nice things with you? Why, universe, why?"

"That is an excellent question," I say, then I drop

the give-him-hell routine and go for the truth. Carter has always been the easiest to talk to about dating. More so than Patrick or even Milo. Carter just wears his heart on his sleeve, the big teddy bear. "...and it turns out, womp, womp, she works for my team now," I say, finishing the story of woe.

He frowns. "Oh, man. That is the worst bad news ever. Almost makes me want to pay for your beer for the rest of time."

That's friendship for you in the face of the universe's seriously rude sense of humor. "I know, and I really like her. Is it weird to like someone that quickly?" I ask as we turn on Abbot Kinney, passing a trendy men's clothing shop.

Carter shoves a hand through his messy hair. "Honestly, I think it's weird if you don't. Especially after two dates. And your first date was all day long. I'd hope you knew you liked her after that much time. It's a vibe thing, you know?"

I nod, glad he gets it. I had a feeling he'd be the right one to talk to. "Yeah, so it sucks that nothing more can happen."

With a hopeful shrug, Carter says, "Maybe in the off-season?"

"She'll still work for the team in the off-season," I point out.

"True, true. I was trying to find a silver lining."

I pat his shoulder. "I appreciate that. But I guess the silver lining is I am going to laser in on football and only football. First game is next weekend. Your sorry ass will be back in San Francisco by then."

"Fuck yes. Gotta get started on my plans for a threepeat," he says, running his fingers through his hair so the sunlight glints off his two rings—his signature move. And hell, I'd do the same if I had even one ring to flash.

"Asshole," I mutter, then we reach the Sunlight Café, a new bowl-centric spot with stark white tables and more kale than a garden patch.

Inside, Maddox orders for us, pays, then sits us down. "When I signed you both, I hardly knew it was a package deal," he teases.

"I like to make things easy for you," Carter says then adopts a too big grin.

Maddox waggles his phone, showing us his Instagram feed. "Nice shot."

"You saw that already?" I ask, kind of amazed.

"You posted it twenty minutes ago," Maddox points out.

"Exactly."

Carter shoots me a knowing look. "Our agent tracks us online. We can't get away with anything." Then to Maddox, he says, "Just kidding. We don't want to get away with anything."

"Good. I like that. Keep being upstanding gentleman and I'll keep inking new deals for you both," he says, then updates me on one of my sponsors before he shifts his attention to my friend.

"Speaking of your partnerships, Date Night is quite sweet on you."

I kick back as Maddox updates my buddy on his partnership with a dating app.

When they're done, Carter says to me in all earnestness, "Drew, when you're ready again, this app is the real deal. For anything. It's all about real romance, real connections—either friendship or love. If you want to meet someone to play ping-pong with, you can. Or to yada yada yada."

"You mean have a *beachside-shave-like* experience," I say in a smoky tone.

Carter cracks up. "You know it."

Maddox turns to me, genuine concern in his dark eyes. "I take it the second date with the woman from last weekend didn't go well."

Carter holds up his hand, like he's going to hold my beer. "I got this, Drew." Then to Maddox, he says, "Turns out she works for the Mercenaries."

My agent winces. "Forbidden love is a tough one," he says, sounding wistful.

Carter tilts his head. "You got a forbidden love story in your past?"

Maddox shakes his head.

"Or did you meet a new dude who's all hot and off-limits?" Carter pushes.

Maddox just dips his head but smiles slyly. "You're not getting any of that out of me."

He's notoriously private about his love life. But a man's choice is a man's choice.

Mine is no dating for now.

My other choice is to send the barber shop pic to Brooke. Once I reach my condo in Santa Monica, I sink onto my couch overlooking the ocean, and I fire it off to her.

Drew: Venice Beach officially has everything now. Sidenote: how cool are we?

Brooke: The coolest. Also, nice shot. You look good.

Good thing I have to get to the field for practice. Otherwise I'd spend the rest of the day texting her.

Wait. Shit. Is this definitely her now?

Drew: Hold on. How do I know this is you?

Brooke: This pic makes my Surf Angel chest flutter.

Drew: Excellent. Let me do another test. Another word for car.

Brooke: You want a McLaren.

Drew: Boat.

Brooke: Yacht. Like your innuendo.

Drew: One more. Another word for shoe?

Brooke: The heels I wore last night. They were black. You wanted them on your shoulders, around your waist, up in the air. Do you believe it's me now?

Drew: A picture is worth a thousand words.

Brooke: If you insist.

Thirty seconds later, a pic lands on my phone, shot from the thighs down. She's wearing a skirt that shows her bare legs, and black heels. Oh Lord have mercy. I want to march over to her office, slam the door, kneel between those creamy thighs, and make her lose her mind with my tongue.

Drew: I'm on my way.

Drew: Just kidding.

Drew: But holy fuck, woman. Your legs should be worshipped. Adored. Kissed. Cherished.

Drew: And then spread wide open so I can spend the afternoon between them.

Brooke: I will never get any work done now.

Nor will I when she sends me another pic. She's hiked up her skirt, and I can just make out the edge of her white lacy panties. I groan, then I take care of business.

A few minutes later, I reply.

Drew: Thought of you the whole time.

Brooke: I'll think of you tonight in bed.

I can't stop. I just can't. When I head to an afternoon practice, I text her some more.

Carter was right. Sometimes you just know.

11

YOUR MOUTH ON MY INNUENDO

Drew

Resisting becomes a bit easier when the season starts the next week. The first game is at home, and we play like a well-oiled machine. I put the team ahead in the second quarter with a forty-yard pass to Clements, who turns that into an absolutely beautiful touchdown.

The crowd goes wild, and the sound of their cheers is such a high. When Clements chest-bumps me on the sidelines, we're both grinning like fools. It's early in the game, but it feels so damn good.

"Nice work, man," I say.

Gabe does a little dance, flexing his biceps. "Told you I'd get it in the end zone. You get it to me, and I'll bust my ass to put that ball where it belongs."

"Sounds like a plan," I say as he kneels and hunts for something under the bench.

When he pops up, he tosses me a red hacky sack. I catch it easily.

"Adams, use your foot," he says, and I hide a smile that he's graduated me to last name familiarity.

"I thought that was your pre-game ritual," I say, pointing out the flaw in his ritual logic.

"Gotta be flexible. Hasn't football taught you anything? I just changed the play. Hacky sack is now our in-game ritual too," he says, then drops the bag toward the ground, kicking it my way with his instep.

When in Rome...

I kick it back.

Maybe he's right about his rituals. They do seem to keep him one hundred ten percent focused. He nails another catch in the third, and our running back, Rand, drives it home on first down.

We finish with a twenty-four to fourteen victory, and it's both a thrill and a relief. After my last year of uncertainty with the Devil Sharks and their payroll slashing, *and* given the Mercenaries' hot mess of a season, the tight game play is all anyone could ask for, the coach included.

"You're looking good, Adams. Keep it up," he says, his voice gruff. It's always gruff—he's such a coach.

"I'll do my best, sir."

After I chat with a sideline reporter, I jog over to the fifty-yard line, beaming when I find my faves in the stands in the seats I snagged for Mom, Mira, Sophie, and Tom.

"Hey, Mom. What did you think?" I say, asking the question I've asked her after every game I've played.

"Loved your focus," she says as she gives me a big hug.

"Any tips?" I ask. That's part of our routine too.

She laughs. "There was less traffic on the way to this stadium, so my tip is keep playing well so we can keep coming here."

"I'll second that," Tom says, then drops a kiss to Mom's forehead. That guy really loves her. It's so good to see.

"Also, the popcorn here is really good," impish Sophie remarks, and I lift her up and onto the field, giving her a big hug.

"I told them to make it special for you," I say.

"I like the pretzels better," Mira weighs in, not to be outdone.

I grab her, hoisting her into my other arm. "Because I said the doubles need the best snacks."

Sophie raises a doubtful brow. "I don't think you did that." She's all stern and serious.

I nod, big and long, staring up at her. "Sure did."

Then Mira nods toward the field. "Can we play now?"

"Maybe later. The grounds crew need to do their

magic to the field, but I can take you out for ice cream if Mom says yes."

They beg her and she gives in, then snaps a pic of me holding them on the edge of the field.

Then, I take them all out for ice cream.

Yeah, I'm glad I was traded across town. I am lucky. I don't want to give this up.

When I post the shot on social that night, captioning it *Celebrating with my faves*, it hardly feels like a good-guy routine. I just love these little stinkers.

The fact that Stephen texts me in the morning to say **Great game, and great shot** is the icing on the cake.

And I do like icing in the form of making him happy.

I'm happy, too, that night when I return home, flop my exhausted body on my couch, and grab the remote to find a movie to watch.

Right when I'm about to click on my Webflix queue, my phone dings with a text.

Brooke: Nice game!

Not gonna lie. I was hoping she'd say something. Truthfully, I was hoping I'd have seen her at the stadium.

Drew: Thanks! Felt good to win the first game. Now I just need to win, oh, say, sixteen more.

Brooke: Um, hello. How about winning all three or four in the post-season too?

Drew: You and your technicalities.

Brooke: Gotta stay on top of details ☺

Ah, hell. That's too tempting.

Drew: I know what I'd like to stay on top of.

That earns me an eye-rolling emoticon.

Drew: I walked right into that. I know. Anyway, were you at the game?

Brooke: I was. I was in the team suite.

Drew: Ooh, fancy!

Brooke: Yes, I wore a suit. So fancy.

Drew: Wait. For real? Also, pics or it didn't happen.

Brooke: I think you have a thing for a sharp-dressed woman.

Drew: You don't have to think that. You should *know* that. That whole boss-lady look from the other night worked for me big time.

Drew: But wait. Hold on. So did your bikini when I met you.

Drew: And the sundress when we got drinks. And the T-shirt after I made you come so hard you saw stars.

Brooke: Cocky much?

Drew: Just all the time.

Drew: But admit it. There were stars?

Brooke: Maybe cosmic dust?

Drew: Well, I better try again then ☺

Brooke: I mean, it's not a bad idea...But seriously, I wore jeans and a nice blouse. And everyone was excited about your performance.

Drew: Did you tell anyone I'm an excellent performer in other ways too?

Brooke: No, Drew. I kept that delicious tidbit to myself.

Drew: If you must.

Brooke: I must.

Drew: I know, but I'm psyched you were there. Too bad you aren't *here* though.

Brooke: Yes, it is too bad. But I was proud of you. What a great game.

Drew: Thanks! Not gonna lie—it feels good to start the season this way. I really want to impress the team and the fans.

Brooke: You absolutely will.

We text a little longer, then we do it again a few days later, then she wishes me luck before I fly to Seattle for an away game. Before I board the flight, I do some interviews with the local media, as per Stephen's request, then do some more in Seattle before the game there. He's keeping me busy, but the chance to talk about the game I love is one I relish.

And I'm happy on Sunday when we win that game in Seattle. As we head off the field, helmets in hand, Gabe hoists the red hacky sack high. "Streak. Don't mess with a streak," he says.

"As if I would."

When I board the plane home a couple of hours later, I text Brooke with *Two in a row!*

And when I land in Los Angeles, my phone serves up her reply.

Brooke: Two in a row! Much better than two-a-day ☺

Drew: Well, not *all* two-a-days.

Brooke: You couldn't resist that either?

Drew: Nope. I could not.

Brooke: I walked into your hardship.

Drew: You could walk right *onto* my hardship too.

Brooke: Drew!

Drew: I meant sit on it. My bad.

Drew: Fuck it. Run over and sit on my face. Then on my hardship.

Brooke: You are the naughtiest.

Drew: Yes, and you're still not sitting on my face or my hardship. But maybe my doorbell will ring when I get home in an hour.

Brooke: I wish I were ringing it...

Drew: And then? Work with me here, woman.

She's quiet for a beat as I make my way past security at the airport, Gabe by my side. His head's bent over his phone. The smile on his face tells me he's likely texting a woman too.

When he looks up, I catch his eye. "Who is she?" I ask.

He just laughs. "Just someone."

"Oh well, thanks for that deep insight."

He shrugs, but his dark eyes are playful. That signature *take-no-prisoners* look has vanished. "Someone I knew long ago."

"Is she the one who got away?" I ask as we reach the street.

"Long ago we never would have been a thing," he says.

"And now?"

His curious look says yes before his mouth says *you never know*.

Once we're in a Lyft, he's back on his phone and I'm on mine, reading Brooke's reply.

Brooke: And then I'd unzip your jeans and get to know your innuendo better.

I haul in a breath. We have a winner. She's feisty tonight.

Drew: I'm in a car with Clements, but just know that later on, when I'm alone, you're going to do unholy things to my innuendo with your mouth.

Brooke: Yes. Yes, I am.

* * *

When I'm home alone, I place an order for Vietnamese noodles from Ding and Dine, then I return to the thread with Brooke.

Drew: Hey. Are you still up?

Brooke: I am. I'm reading a book. Almost done with it though.

Drew: Is it good?

Brooke: Terrific. It's the new Axel Huxley.

Drew: He's my cousin!

Brooke: For real?

Drew: I swear on my right arm. He lives in New York, and he's scowly, and sarcastic, and funny as fuck.

Brooke: Talented too.

Drew: Well, yeah, that. I finished his newest a couple weeks ago. Good stuff! (Well, I listened to the audio. Does that count?)

Brooke: Why would it not count? Of course it counts.

Drew: Some people think that doesn't count.

Brooke: Some people are jackasses.

Drew: True words.

Brooke: Are you home now?

Drew: Yup. Just ordered some food. I'm hungry. But I'm no good in the kitchen.

Brooke: I'll teach you someday ☺

I wish we were having that someday now—for the cooking, and the hardships, and the talking.

Since we keep talking for another hour.

12

HARSHING ON MUFFINS

Drew

On Wednesday night, I catch up with Patrick in Santa Monica for dinner. Maddox recommended a new Indian food truck for us to try, and since it's in my neighborhood this week, I leave my condo and head out to meet Patrick.

But when I'm a block away from our meet-up, I spot Ruby's Taco Truck before the Indian truck. My doubt-meter spikes once I spy Patrick chatting with the guy at the window.

Why do I think my buddy's going to milk the whole *taco spankings* thing?

Oh, because he has.

The fucker has sent me several gifts in the last few weeks.

First, the day after the ultimate text trick, as he called it, he sent licorice to my home along with this text. *Bought some licorice tonight, hottie. I'm practicing hitting myself with it. But they keep breaking. Got any tips?*

Hit yourself harder, I'd replied.

The day after my first win, he sent an order of pancakes to my house with syrup on the side, along with a text: *I wore these today on my tits. Hope you love your brekkie, hot-stuff stud-muffin.*

I ate the pancakes. They were tasty. But not as tasty as getting back at him by snapping a picture of myself on the beach with a clown and tagging it with his name—*Hanging with my finance wizard, Patrick.*

I'm waiting for the next installment. It's got to be coming tonight. This taco truck has *setup* written all over it.

He strides over to me, whipping off his aviator shades. They complete the look he's working—the pressed pants, the polished shoes, and the tailored white shirt. He probably came from the office. By contrast, I'm in jeans, a T-shirt, and a ball cap.

He flashes me a grin. "Two in a row, man. That's the way to do it."

Hmm. I'm not picking up on a prankster vibe. I peer around. "Did you bring a bag of skittles? You'll give me some then say you licked them all?"

He pulls a face like that's ridic. "Who has time for that?"

"Fair point."

I glance at the yellow truck. "Did you hire a stripper to jump out of a giant taco while wielding a starter spanking kit?"

Patrick scoffs. "Starter? I'd figured advanced for you. Also, don't try to guess my next move. This won't end. Ever. And you don't want it to."

Truth. We've played so many pranks on each other over the years that it's our love language. "But when I can predict your next move, I win the round," I say, seizing a chance to take control of the game. I do like control—almost as much as I love winning.

"Fair enough," Patrick says, then clears his throat, nodding to the nearby truck. "In all seriousness, the owner of Ruby's Taco Truck loves you. I had lunch here the other day, and you came up. Hope you don't mind if we skip the Maddox rec and go here? The tacos are huge. You only need one."

Boom. I spot my opening. "Hold on. You just reminded me I forgot to reply to Maddox's last text."

I grab my phone, and type out a quick message and send it, but not to my agent.

Rejoining the conversation, I tell Patrick, "Tacos sound great. Just make sure it's big enough for me."

"That's what she said," he quips without missing a beat.

I smirk, feeling smug. "Check your texts, asshole."

He does, and his eyes widen as he lets out a long

"Fuuuuuck" as he reads my note to him: *You're going to say this in five seconds.*

I blow on my fingernails. "Don't forget I play to win."

"You bastard," he mutters.

"You mean you fucking steely-eyed, brilliant bastard who just schooled you in your game?"

"Yes," he grumbles, then adds, "I'm not worthy."

"That is true. But I'll treat you to tacos anyway."

We reach the truck, which features an illustration of a Chihuahua holding a big taco. "Is that the owner's dog?"

Patrick nods. "Yup. Roman's pup is Ruby. She has a dog bed attached on the side of the truck. That way she won't get in the way of the food, but she can hang with Roman."

I walk around the truck, smiling when I spot the cute min-pin critter sleeping in a comfy-looking bed. I snap a shot of the truck and send it to Milo in New York. He's obsessed with his pooch too, and his dog goes to work with him every day at his bike shop.

When I return to Patrick, he says, "Roman will probably want a selfie with you. You cool with that?"

"Always," I say.

"Good. I figured the team would be happy as well, since they love your good-guy-about-town image. They released some shots of you from that charity thing you did the other week."

I don't follow that stuff too closely, but I know

Maddox does, and if there were a problem, he'd have told me. Still, I'm curious. "What sort of shots?"

"Just you shaking hands, chatting with donors and such. Oh, and like you asked me to, I got in touch with the org about you doing volunteer work and making a donation." He confirms the amount we discussed and suggests we meet with Paul. "You're still good with that?"

"Absolutely. Thanks for making that happen."

"And that was a nice shot of you and the babe from the front office," he says offhand as we move up in line.

Wait. Hold the hell on. "What do you mean?" I ask cautiously.

"You and the blonde. There was a shot of the two of you in front of the banner," he says, and instantly, I relax.

"Oh, cool. Yeah, she's fun to chat with. We're buds," I say, not quite making eye contact.

Carter's the only one who's privy to the full truth. But there's no reason to tell Patrick the details since nothing is going on with Brooke and me. And he doesn't know Brooke is my IOU. He thinks the woman I was texting was just a random hookup.

It's better that way. If I tell him, he'll worry. He has ever since college when I was involved with Marie my senior year. The guy has never forgotten what went down when I dated her, so I don't need to stress him out until there's something to tell.

I shake off my worries, too, when we reach the window and Patrick drops a hand to my shoulder and introduces me to Roman.

A tattooed but baby-faced burly man extends his hand from behind the window. "Good to meet you. Big fan. Whatever you want. It's on the house."

"Thanks, man, but I'm more than happy to pay for your fine food. And I appreciate the compliment."

"And I'd appreciate it if you could bring a ring to Los Angeles," he says with a wry smile.

"I will absolutely do my best," I say, and when the food is ready, Roman refuses the cash, so I stuff a fifty in the tip jar.

Roman grabs his phone, and we smile for the camera.

After we eat, Patrick and I wander along Ocean Avenue. When we near the old parking garage, that was converted into a movie theater, my gaze snags on the marquee for Silver Screen Theater. A wave of nostalgia crashes into me. "It's tonight. *Fake Play*."

I'd forgotten the showing was this evening.

Patrick knits his brow in question. "That old flick?"

"That old flick is a good flick, man." I check the time. It's almost seven. Perfect.

"You and your love of old movies," he says, shaking his head, amused.

"Me and my love of old movies are going in. See you later."

I give Patrick a tip of the cap, and head for the ticket counter, when he calls out, "Dude, I'm going with you."

I arch an eyebrow. "To see *that old flick*? I don't want to cramp your new, flashy style."

"I'll just pretend I don't know you. It'll be fine."

"Too bad I was going to treat. Not so sure I will now," I say as I slap some bills at the counter and buy the tickets anyway. I like to treat, especially after college.

"Now I do owe you," he says with a smirk as we head into the lobby.

"I'll be sure to send a clown to collect."

He growls. "You wouldn't."

"I might," I say as I catch sight of a woman at the popcorn counter who looks a lot like Brooke.

And then...Brooke.

Wowzers.

She wears a pink sundress and strappy sandals. Her hair falls loosely over her tanned shoulders.

She must be with her sister.

Brooke's eyes catch mine and she smiles warmly —a colleague smile, but that's cool. "Hey, Adams," Brooke says, using my last name like most people in the organization do. "Good to see you."

"And you too," I say, going along with the *just friends* bit.

I mean, we are *friends-ish.*

The last few weeks of dirty texting aside.

Brooke gestures to the woman next to her. "This is my sister. Cara."

"And you two must be the guys planning clown pranks," Cara says with an *I-caught-you* expression.

Patrick adopts a serious look as he eyes Brooke's sister. "For the record, I am vehemently opposed to clown pranks. And to clowns."

Cara nods sagely. "I get that."

"Well, clearly this was meant to be," he says with a smile now.

Cara laughs, then she gestures to the theater. "Are you two clowns heading to see *Fake Play*?"

Patrick nods. "We are." Then, with a lingering glance Cara's way, he says, "Would you like to sit together? That way, if there are clowns or anything in the flick, we can support each other through it."

She sets a hand on her chest. "That'd be great." Cara turns to Brooke, raising her eyebrows in question. "Does that work for you?"

"Works for me," Brooke says.

Patrick goes to the counter, picks up the cost of the air-popped popcorn Brooke was buying as well as one for himself, and then hands her the bucket. Patrick and Cara chit-chat the whole time.

Brooke and I are quiet, but our eyebrow arches and knowing looks are their own language, saying *well, those two hit it off quickly.*

As we enter the movie theater, I drop back, letting Patrick and Cara walk in front of us. "That was fast," I say, nodding to them.

"It was. Tell me he's a good guy," she says, her tone deadly serious, her jaw tight.

I hold up my hand as if taking an oath. "He's like a brother. I trust him with my life."

"I will *hurt* anyone who hurts my sister. I don't care if those two just met. If he does her wrong..."

I squeeze her shoulder in reassurance. "I swear. Also, he's petrified of clowns, so he definitely needs the protection."

She seems to relax under my touch and from my words. I lean into Brooke, drawing a quick inhale of her sexy, sunshine scent. "By the way, you look amazing," I whisper, low, just for her. No harm in a little compliment.

"So do you," she whispers.

"What were the chances we'd run into each other here?" I ask as we head down the aisle.

"Pretty good, technically. Considering we talked about this being our favorite movie, and it's only playing tonight."

"Okay, then. So those are damn good odds," I say with a smile. "But I swear, I wasn't stalking you. It was...serendipity."

Her smile is magical. "Let's go with that."

Patrick stops at a middle row and heads in first.

Cara follows, then Brooke, then me. What a fantastic impromptu seating chart.

Brooke offers me some of her popcorn. "I know you like food. Want to share?"

"I'm always hungry." I take her up on her offer and grab a handful. But before I crunch into the kernels, I ask, "Any idea where I could get a great risotto?"

"My kitchen," she whispers.

I flash back to that night with her, kissing her while she was cooking. Damn. I wish we'd had that second date. Glancing across at Patrick, I confirm he's busy then lean closer to Brooke, stealing a moment. "In our parallel universe, I'm back in your kitchen."

"Wow. You *are* hungry," she teases.

"I sure am."

She adopts a thoughtful look. "Am I making... eggplant parmesan?"

"You're doing *something* with an eggplant," I say. "As far as I'm concerned, you hold eggplant power over me. Zucchini too."

"Ooh, I love zucchini in a pasta primavera."

I breathe an over-the-top sigh of relief. "I'm so glad you didn't say zucchini muffins."

"Muffins should be abolished."

"Right? What's the point of muffins? They don't know if they want to be bread or dessert." I'd planned on dirty-talking her with a scenario of kissing her in her kitchen, and now we're harshing on muffins.

But I'm a happy camper.

"If I want a cupcake," she says, "I'll have a cupcake and I'll frost it, thank you very much."

"Just pick a side, muffins," I say.

Brooke peeks over at Patrick and Cara, who look like they might be wearing sandwich boards for insta-love, then leans a little closer to me, her hair swishing over my shoulder. "You're back in my kitchen too. I'm up on the counter," she whispers.

Yes. Let's do this. "I'm lifting your skirt."

"I've got my hands on your shoulders."

"You're pushing me down," I say.

A small gasp falls from her mouth. "So you can work on your deal."

"I will work very hard on my deal."

Brooke closes her eyes and inhales sharply. When she opens them, those brown irises glimmer with heat.

"We should have cupcakes later," I suggest.

She nibbles on her lower lip, then smiles wickedly as the opening credits begin.

13

JUST A TROUBLEMAKER

Drew

When the movie ends, Patrick and Cara walk ahead, gabbing the whole way out. Once we're on Ocean Avenue, I'm not surprised at all when my friend suggests, "Want to grab a beer? Shave ice? Smoothie?"

The question's directed at the group but I know who it's really for. He's a goner already. Maybe Cara is too, because she chimes in with an enthused, "Definitely."

But Brooke yawns rather than answers.

"It's past your bedtime," Cara teases. "It's already nine."

"Yes, someone has been working early and late,"

Brooke says, with another yawn. "But I don't mind if you want to stay."

"I'll drive you home," Cara says brightly. Maybe she feels guilty that she wanted to stay since they're sharing a car.

"I'll drive you, Brooke," I offer. "My car's nearby."

Cara's big eyes widen more. "You don't mind?"

"I don't mind at all," I say, my poker face tight.

Brooke turns away from me, but she's smiling. "Thanks. That's sweet of you."

Venice is about four miles away. But in Los Angeles, that trip could take fifteen minutes or an hour.

Good thing I like the company.

"So, are you really tired?" I ask as I open the passenger side door to my car in the parking garage.

Brooke shoots me a coy look. "What do you think?"

With a lopsided grin, I walk around to the driver's side. "You little enabler," I tease as I start the car and back out.

"Well, have you ever seen two people hit it off so fast?"

"It was pretty instant. Just add clown phobia and popcorn."

She laughs. "Cara hasn't dated anyone in a long

time. She's been so focused on school and classes. But those two had that *bam!* chemistry."

"I think I know what that's like," I say.

"Me too," she says as I exit the garage and pull onto the street.

And right into traffic.

Of course there's traffic at nine-fifteen on a Wednesday night.

"Sorry, Drew," she says. "I should have taken a Lyft."

I slice that notion off at the knees. "Do I look like I don't want to spend time with you?"

She smiles, apologetic. "But this is bad," she says, gesturing to the long slog of cars ahead of us.

"I did offer," I say as I slow even more at a light. "And I know what this town is like. Besides, I figure we need to do our movie review for *Fake Play.*"

That earns me a grin. Nothing apologetic in it at all. "Well, a fake romance between the quarterback and the girl next door is hard to resist," she says with a wistful sigh. "It *only* works because he's so enchanted with her but takes forever to realize it."

I let that sink in for a moment. "Huh. I never saw it that way."

"You don't?"

"I think he knows from the start that she revs his engine, and that's why he suggests her when his agent says he needs a fake date."

Brooke holds up a finger to make a point. "*But* he

only realizes he's attracted to her. He's sort of delight-fully clueless that he's falling for her."

She has a point, but I still think the hero was into her for a long time. "I think it just took him an age to say it out loud. It's funny how two people can see the same film and take away different things from it."

"It is. I also notice different aspects of the story now that I'm older."

"For sure. When I first saw it as a middle schooler, I just loved the football scenes. The romance part was way over my head," I admit, then furrow my brow. "Maybe my younger self was protecting me. I did see it with my mom."

"Is she a movie fan too?"

I tap the gas lightly, scooting a car length ahead. "Sure is. Movies were our guilty pleasure growing up. It was just the two of us, and we tried to hit all the big releases. The superhero flicks, the talking dog movies, the PG romances, the adventure tales. She made air-popped popcorn and tucked a Ziploc bag of it in her purse."

Brooke laughs. "I love her already. Smart woman with her big-purse life hack."

"I used to tease her that she could carry a tent in her purse, and she'd say, *You think I don't have one in there already?*"

"Do you still go with her to the movies?"

"Sometimes. I try to take the twins too, when I go, though it's tough during the season. I took them a lot during the off-season. I can pretty much sing any song from any animated princess flick."

"'Let My Hair Down,'" Brooke says, firing off the signature tune from a Rapunzel remake.

I scoff, then sing the opening lines.

Brooke claps in approval. "Well done."

"Why, thank you very much," I say.

"Now, speaking of your mom, I have to know— does she call you Andrew a lot?" Brooke asks as we cruise along another block. "You said she was the only one who called you that, but only when you were in trouble."

"I was a troublemaker growing up, Brooke. Don't let this sweet face fool you." I give her a smoldering grin that's not at all sweet.

"Maybe you still are?" she asks with an arch in her brow and a hint of sultry in her voice.

"Maybe I am," I say, sensing an invitation in the air between us. It crackles with the same energy as when we met.

The same energy that's damn hard to resist.

The car in front of me slows. I try to peer around the cars ahead to get a read on the situation. But it's kind of pointless in this city.

I turn to Brooke, and she's nibbling on her lip again. Dirty thoughts seem to flicker across her brown eyes as she says, "How are you a troublemaker these days?"

Fuck holding back. "I want to get into all kinds of

trouble with you," I say as I turn my gaze fully to her, my eyes roaming up and down her sexy frame. When our eyes lock, heat flares between us and I'm rumbling her name. "Brooke."

"Drew," she whispers, her voice threaded with desire.

"Do you like trouble?"

Her breath seems to catch, then she nods shakily. "A lot. Especially right now."

"Same here."

I lift my hand, reach for her face, and cup her cheek. She gasps, and before either one of us can say another word—before I can evaluate or analyze—I dip my mouth to hers and kiss those delicious lips. Her tongue darts out, and she nips me back, running her teeth along my bottom lip, and out of nowhere a quick kiss turns into a hot, dirty one.

A car horn honks behind us, and we pull apart. But the white sedan in front of me has only moved ten feet. I drive slowly, running one hand along Brooke's leg, down to the edge of her dress. My fingers play at the hem, and she murmurs as we slink along at a snail's pace. My eyes drift to her legs, so toned and strong. The whole look she's working tonight is killing me.

Maybe one touch will satisfy me.

Or maybe I'm just a troublemaker.

I inch my finger under her skirt. She lets her knees fall open the slightest bit.

It's an RSVP to trouble and I take it. "I'm not feeling friendly toward you whatsoever," I rasp.

She's quiet for a beat, then she whispers, "Don't be friendly."

And I run with it.

My fingers travel up the soft flesh of her thighs. Then, higher still.

She tugs her skirt up farther, then spreads her legs.

14

THE GOOD KIND OF TROUBLE

Brooke

Surrounded by cars but totally alone behind tinted windows, this is trouble, but the good kind.

I've never done anything like this. I've had a hard enough time coming with a guy in bed, so I've never tried to steal an O out of the boudoir. But when Drew touches me, I feel daring.

The man is focused on me, on helping me *finally* get out of my head.

His fingers slide along the damp panel of my panties, then he flashes a wicked grin as he slips one under, rubbing against my wetness. I arch into him.

"Oh, honey, I've missed this," he says in a dirty purr.

"Me too," I admit, my breath coming fast.

"Traffic rocks," he says, as he paints dizzying strokes up and down my center.

My hips seek out his hand.

I spread my legs wider.

A rumble escapes his lips. "Yeah, do that. Love seeing you get so turned on you spread your legs for me."

His dirty words are a charge, as if someone plugged me in, and I'm now electrified. The pleasure builds, rippling across my skin.

He drags a finger down me slowly, then brings it to his lips and sucks off the taste. "Fucking delicious," he murmurs as he returns to me.

I whimper as he strokes.

"If we weren't stuck in traffic, I'd go down on you." His voice husky. "Bury my face between those pretty legs."

"I'd grab your hair, pull you close," I say, getting into the scene.

"You'd fuck my face hard—wrap your heels nice and tight around me, and I'd devour you," he says in a low, dirty growl.

I'm lost. I'm absolutely lost as he touches me, faster and impossibly faster still. Every muscle tenses blissfully as an orgasm charges through me.

I cry out as I come undone in his car.

When the release subsides, I blink my eyes open, and wow.

Suddenly, the cars are moving. Traffic is unstuck.

Drew licks his fingers once more then grips the wheel, navigating through moving traffic like a pro. "Maybe you have superpowers. One orgasm and you broke through the traffic jam."

"Just call me Miss O," I say, breathless.

A satisfied smile lights his handsome face. "By the way," he says, his tone full of pride and happiness, "I still owe you."

"You do," I say with a dopey grin. Only, I'm not thinking about my pleasure. I'm thinking about his. "But I owe you too."

"I can think of a few ways you can repay me."

In less than ten minutes, we're at my house.

He's right behind me as I close the door to the world, taking our brand of trouble inside.

We collide in my living room. His hands grab my face. His mouth hunts mine ruthlessly. My hands are busy too. I grip his hard-on over his jeans, then quickly unbutton and unzip the denim.

I free his cock.

"Ahhh, yes," he mutters the second I clasp my hand around his dick.

I shudder at the feel of his hot, pulsing length, at how turned on he is. I play with him, relishing each tight stroke of my fist along his shaft. I'm dying to wrap my lips around him.

I indulge, dropping to my knees, pushing his jeans down his thighs as I go.

I kiss the head. The sound he makes is animalistic.

"Fuck, Brooke, that feels good," he says, all throaty and deep.

His words spur me on. With him I feel daring, and that's new for me. All day, I'm the cautious one, the woman who reads on the beach rather than riding the waves. But Drew unlocks the gambler in me. My thumb slides over the head of his dick, and I swipe off a drop of his arousal, then spread it over my top lip.

He growls. "Yes, you look so goddamn sexy," he praises, then wraps his hand tighter around my head. "Now suck my dick. You know you fucking want to."

His mouth is the most exciting thing that's ever happened to my sex life. When he unfurls filthy phrases from his lips, I let go of the racing loop of thoughts about my day, about work, about bills. I want to say the dirty words too—such a contrast to the legal ones I write and speak all day.

"You taste so good," I say as I return to his cock.

"And you look so hot on your knees."

As I draw him deeper, I cup his balls, squeezing gently.

"Yeah, do that again," he hisses.

I obey, fondling his balls, then stroking the base of his cock. He pulses in my mouth, and I savor him, sucking and delighting in his dick. Because his dick *is* an absolute delight. Thick and hard and eager.

Have I ever enjoyed giving head so much? No. I don't think so. This is new too, and my core aches as I lick him. My mind crackles as I suck his shaft.

"Now, lick the head. Tease me with that wicked tongue," he commands, and I follow his orders, flicking my tongue over his crown.

I grow wetter with everything he says, and soon, I'm rocking my hips as I go to town on his cock.

"Been wanting to fuck that sweet mouth of yours since the day I met you," he murmurs, and pleasure pulses hot in my center.

For a second, I let him fall from my lips. "So do it."

Shaking his head, he reaches for my shoulders, pulls me up, and kisses my lips. "Need to fuck you right now. Get on your hands and knees."

God. Yes. Now.

Spinning around, I stumble over to the couch and get on the cushions, lifting my skirt.

He grabs a condom from his wallet, sheaths his cock, then kneels behind me, positioning himself at my entrance.

"Please, fuck me hard," I say, my temperature spiking as I talk too. I think I'm discovering my kink with Drew.

He shoves deep inside me with a long, possessive growl.

"Yesssss," he murmurs.

My kink is words.

Dirty, delicious words said to me. Said *by* me.

That first night he unlocked something inside my body. Now, my mind is getting in on it too. I'm connecting all the dots to discover the way I crave him in bed.

I crave his body and his mouth.

He grips my hips, and he delivers on his promise. With long, deep thrusts, he fucks me hard.

Pleasure twists inside me in a fiery swirl as I brace myself on my palms. Ideas flash before me in a heated reel.

"Smack my ass," I say, taking another chance.

"Fuck yes," he growls, raising a hand and swatting the fuck out of me.

Oh!

That hurts so good.

"Again," I urge, craning my neck to watch him. It's erotic and wicked as he lifts that strong arm, raises that big hand, and his palm connects with my flesh again.

It stings, but the pain radiates straight to my core, thrumming through my clit.

"More," I beg.

Again and again, he swats me, cheek to cheek. "You like that? You like it hard and rough?"

"I do," I pant as I spiral into a wild, crescendo.

Electricity flares in me, then throbs in my center.

One more hard smack. I fly off the cliff, losing my mind to this moment.

Seconds later, he's nailing me, and it's intense, so intense I'm not sure I can withstand the pleasure.

He's groaning, mumbling *oh fuck, yes, so good*.

Then he slams into me on a deep, dizzying thrust and roars, "Yes, fucking yes."

A new wave of pleasure crests as if a heightened aftershock of my own orgasm mingles with his. Is that a thing? As I curl my toes, it feels like a thing.

Everything feels wild and passionate as we pant and moan.

I'm not sure I'll ever float down from this high. But there's a new high coming my way when he gently moves my face so he can press a tender kiss to my lips. Then the back of my neck.

Now my hair. "Be right back," he whispers.

When he eases out and heads to the kitchen to toss the condom, I sink onto my side on the couch.

A few seconds later, he returns, his jeans pulled up but still undone. His hair is a mess. His clothes too. But his lopsided grin makes my heart squeeze.

I pat the couch. "Stay."

He flops next to me. "I want to."

"Because you want me to cook for you," I tease.

His expression turns fully earnest as he shakes his head. "I like your cooking. But I really like you."

My heart squeezes harder. "Same here," I say.

That is the real trouble.

15

TEACH ME

Drew

This hardly feels like a bad idea—hanging out in her home, helping her cook.

And since I don't want to leave our parallel universe yet, I yank open the fridge and declare, "I want to help you. Give me orders."

Brooke wiggles her brows. "You want me to turn the tables on you in the kitchen?"

I tap my chin, giving her a doubtful stare. "Woman, I believe you gave me orders in the bedroom too. Need I remind you of your demands? *Smack my ass. Fuck me hard*, and so on," I say as she reaches for some asparagus from the crisper.

She stops mid-grab. "Hmm. That's a fair point. I'll

continue bossing you around, Mister O Dealer," she says.

I pat my chest. "I delivered two tonight, so I'm feeling pretty good," I say as she sets the veggies on the counter, then reaches for a carton of tofu.

"Guess what? So am I," she says in a sultry purr.

"Good. You deserve to. In the real world and in our parallel universe," I say.

She tosses me a soft smile, but it's a little poignant, recognizing that we're stealing this night together.

Pretending this could be us.

But I'm not in the mood for a world where being together is a risk. "How are you such a good cook? Gimme details," I say.

"Necessity. Mom and Dad worked late a lot, so I learned to cook for Cara and me in high school."

"Sandwiches wouldn't do? Or frozen food?"

She shudders as she crosses to the nearby pantry. "No way. Mom and Dad were foodies before foodies were a thing," she says as she grabs a can of chick-peas. "They'd have flipped their lids if I made sand-wiches. Plus, I liked taking care of Cara."

"That tracks. You were a mama bear tonight at the movies. But a softie too."

Her nose crinkles as she sets the can on the counter. "That describes me to a T where she's involved." Then she points to the cupboard beneath the stove. "Your first order. Grab the frying pan."

"Same one you used the first time I was here?" I ask.

"I'll be impressed if you can identify a pan," she says, doubtful.

"Prepare to be impressed," I say, bending to open the cupboard, then rooting around for it. Boom. Got it. I waggle the pan. "I told you—I'm multi-talented."

"Yes, your pan identification skills are top-notch," she says, setting it on the stove but not turning on the heat.

"So, growing up you had to learn to cook," I say, returning to the conversation.

"I did, but somewhere along the way, something surprising happened," she says, an impish grin on her face as she snags a bottle of olive oil from a cabinet, stretching to reach it. Mmm. The view. The delicious view of her exposed back as her tank top rises. She's wearing sleep shorts too, and the whole casual just-been-fucked look is turning me on again.

But I'll have to service my stomach first. "What's the surprise? Also, order me around to find the can opener."

"Drawer next to the stove. And the surprise is I learned to love cooking," she says with a casual shrug. "It's fun for me now. I find it both challenging and relaxing."

"Like a recipe is a puzzle?" I ask as I rinse the top of the can then open it.

"Exactly." She grabs a cutting board from the

counter. "You hope it'll turn out the way you intended, but you never quite know."

"Sounds a lot like a football play."

She gives an approving smile. "It kind of is. And sometimes you have to call an audible."

That's speaking my language. "Cooking and football. I love it. What's next? Teach me to cook like we talked about. I want to learn."

"It's all about the knife," she says, spinning around to snag one from the knife block, then wielding the sharp blade.

"Got it. Good knives rule."

"And a little seasoning goes a long way," she adds as she sets the asparagus on the cutting board and chops a few stalks. But she stops mid slice. "Wait. You were raised by a single mom. She never taught you to cook?"

I wag a finger. "Brooke. Did you just assume all single moms cook?"

She holds up a *down, boy* hand. "No. I make no assumptions. But your mom raised a smart, thoughtful man, who holds doors for women and calls when he says he will, so I *deduce* she taught you life skills, like laundry and how to balance a bank account," she says, returning to her chopping.

I waggle my fingers toward the knife. "My turn. I learn by doing."

She hands me the utensil.

I slide in next to her and take over chopping the

asparagus. "Mom did teach me. Or rather, she tried to teach me, but I was a sports-obsessed, high-energy kid, so guess what happened at dinnertime?"

"She sent you out to race around the block?" she asks as she turns on the stove, drizzles some olive oil in the pan.

"Welcome to my childhood. I was like a dog who needed to be run." I finish the asparagus, then nod toward the frying pan. "Just drop it in?"

"You got it, handsome." She takes over, sautéing the asparagus with some pre-cut tofu. "Why don't you grab some pepper and salt? Top cabinet to the right."

"Just pepper and salt?" I ask as I comply.

"Sometimes simple is best."

"Like hanging out here in your house with you," I say, and wow. I sound like a lust-struck fool.

But I don't mind.

Ten minutes later, we finish cooking, and together we plate the food, grab some drinks, then sit at her counter.

She hands me a bottle of pale ale, then pours herself some chardonnay. "To trouble," she says, raising the glass to toast. "Our parallel universe full of good, dirty trouble."

"I'll drink to that," I say, my chest tingling at those words. After our toast, I take a bite and moan. "Damn, I'm a good cook."

She laughs. "It's all you, Drew."

"Maybe I had a little help," I concede. "Now, tell me more about you and Cara."

"Because Patrick is sweet on her?"

I scoff. "I'm not his keeper. He can be sweet on whoever he wants. I want to know more about her because"—I stop, lean closer, and dust a kiss to her cheek—"I'm into her sister. I want to know more about the important people in your life."

She dips her face, then purses her lips like she's hiding a smile. As we eat, she tells me more about their antics growing up. She asks about my sisters and I chat about them.

Then, I ask if she's liking her new job. "Is the promotion what you want?"

"It is. I love it. Checking out contracts, looking for loopholes and technicalities. It's just my speed."

"That's so very you," I say.

"It is. I'm still a little shocked I got the job," she says.

"I'm not. You're brilliant," I say.

She blushes. "I just mean because it's such a good gig. Working for Carlisle Enterprises has always been a bit of a dream. It's sort of the perfect amount of lawyering for me. No courtrooms," she says with a self-deprecating laugh.

"Not your style?"

"No way. I like the details of law, the puzzle of law, but I don't want to go fight or roll the dice," she says.

Another thirty minutes of talk passes in a flash as

we get to know each other and continues as we're cleaning up. How is this only our second night together when we already have such a natural rhythm and flow?

But then, it's not entirely our second night. We spent the meet-and-greet together—chastely—and then walked around together. We've texted for weeks.

But every time I see her, one moment seems to spill into the next. She's got to be feeling the same pull, despite the risks.

"By the way," I say, "you said earlier that I was a man of his word. I'm glad you're not holding that ghosting against past-me anymore," I say as I close the dishwasher.

"Drew," she says, sounding as if she's coming clean about something. "Some of my emotions that night weren't even because of you," she says, then blows out a breath. "My ex cheated on me with many women. He even messaged me the day I met you, so that was in my head. So when I thought I hadn't heard from you...it all seemed too good to be true."

My heart hurts for her, but I also want to give a piece of my mind to the dumb shit who cheated on her. "He didn't deserve you," I bite out. "He doesn't deserve anyone."

"That's probably true. But I wanted to apologize. I should have...trusted our first night together and tried harder to track you down. Cara even suggested it."

I straighten with interest at that last nugget. "She knows about us?"

"I told her, yeah. But she won't say anything to Patrick. She knows that guy talk belongs in the sister vault."

"Good. I haven't said anything to him," I admit, but then I wave off any concerns. "Just because he'd worry, since he's my finance guy and all. He takes an interest in all my business affairs, so he might worry about..."

Fuck. I hate saying this out loud.

"How it would look," she supplies, her tone heavy. She leans back against the counter, her mood clearly dampened.

Patrick's concerns are more than appearances though. If I tell him about Brooke too soon, he'll worry it'd be college all over again, like when I fell for Marie.

But the situation with Brooke isn't the same. Not one bit. "Yes," I say, but then I try to brighten the mood. "But my buddy Carter knows. I kinda couldn't keep it from him."

"Why's that?" She sounds delighted, and I'm glad for the one eighty.

"He's a giant cinnamon roll," I say. "He even suggested we date in the off-season," I say impulsively. I didn't plan to put that possibility out there tonight, but maybe it's not the worst idea? Maybe there is a way to pull *us* off.

She lifts a curious brow. "He did?"

"Probably nutty?" I suggest with a light laugh in case I'm coming on too strong. "But maybe not?"

She exhales hard. "I don't know. What I do know is Stephen loves the good-guy image you have. He's been so pleased with your press coverage, your social media. I mean, obviously he's impressed with your game play, but he likes the whole package. I don't want to ruin it."

My hope deflates. Maybe that was too wild an idea.

"But," she adds, like she's reconsidering it, "it's something to think about."

I smile. I don't try to hold it back. "Yeah?"

She reaches for my hand. Clasps tight. "Yeah. Let's...*think about it*."

I should be focusing on football, but two games into the season and I'm kicking ass. Maybe that's a sign I can somehow manage...*something* with Brooke.

She squeezes my hand, then adds, "I like that you told him, then."

"It's impossible not to. He knows everything. He helped me deal with my last relationship when it imploded," I say, since we're having some kind of confessional night.

"What happened? May I ask?" She lets go of my hand and lifts her wine from the counter to finish the last sip.

"Of course you can. The last woman I dated was

always taking selfies with me at games, and kind of parading me around when we went out. Talking me up for my role on the team. Sort of made me feel like she wasn't actually into me." I feel a little foolish as I share the story. But that's how I felt at the time. "There's this fine line between *are you using me for your business,* and *do you just enjoy taking selfies?* I worried I'd sound like a dick, so I probably stayed with her longer than I should have. And when I finally got out, there was a big scene. She yelled at me in the hallway of my building, and it was just..."

She frowns in sympathy as she sets the wineglass in the sink. "A hot mess?"

"Exactly. It happened during the off-season, and I sort of needed to escape for a while. Carter and I took off for New York and hung out with friends there just to get away. That probably sounds ridiculous."

She shakes her head, her eyes thoughtful. "Not at all. That makes sense. Sometimes, we just need a break. I get it." She takes a beat, tilts her head. "Is that another reason why you kept quiet about who you were at first?"

"Definitely," I say, glad to be truthful with her. I only like games on the football field—and the good kind in the bedroom. "But I really enjoyed not talking football with you. I like that we can talk about anything."

"Me too," she says.

The clock on the wall ticks closer to eleven, interrupting us.

Or maybe giving me an opportunity. "Brooke," I begin, gearing up to ask to stay.

Her shoulders tense. Her jaw tightens.

Oh, shit? Does she think I want to take off? "Honey, it's not bad," I say.

"I didn't think it was," she says, then she lifts her fingers to her temple and rubs.

"Are you okay?"

"Just a tiny start of a headache."

"You get headaches? Sophie does. Those are brutal."

"Migraines. I wouldn't wish it on anyone."

"What makes it feel better? A hot shower? A massage?"

"Both?" she says, a little excited.

I seize the chance to make her feel better. "Then let's do it."

A couple minutes later, we're under the stream of water in her shower, and I'm rubbing her neck and her shoulders, and she's murmuring then moaning as I rub.

I keep it up for as long as she needs. Until she says, "I think you scared it away. Maybe you do have superpowers."

"Traffic cowers in the presence of your orgasms and migraines hide in the face of my hands," I say as she turns off the shower, and we step out.

"I'm glad I don't have to take a migraine pill. They make me dizzy and a little out of it," she says, but then she yawns while drying off.

"Let's get you to bed," I say wrapping a towel around my waist.

"Sleep with me." She sounds more vulnerable than she has before.

She's such a strong, tough woman, but she's showing me tender sides tonight.

I want more of them.

"I will," I say, and curl up under the covers with her.

In the morning, I'm still thinking about the off-season, wishing it were sooner.

Wondering what we can pull off.

16

MY BIGGEST FAN

Drew

That weekend we hit the road again, but actually it's the highway across town to play the Devil Sharks.

Before the game, I wonder if playing on my old turf will throw me off. Turns out, the answer is no. They're a shell of a team, and we win by a delightfully embarrassing amount.

The Mercenaries are now three for three. This doesn't feel like luck. It feels like talent and hard work paying off.

Brooke and I text every day and talk too, so much that I can't stop thinking about February.

So much that on Wednesday morning, after I lace up my sneakers and I hit the beach as the sun rises, I call Carter. He's the one person I need to talk to.

My buddy answers on FaceTime with a big yawn and a close-up of his pie hole. "Dude, you woke me up," he grumbles, sounding like he just got out of bed.

"Dude, I know you're at the gym."

With a scowl, he pulls back the angle, and I see he's climbing the StairMaster. "Fine, fine. You know I'm an early bird. Anyway, I won't give you tips on the Las Vegas Pioneers. We kicked their ass last weekend because we are the best team in the league. But hey, good luck when you face them."

"Thanks," I say drily as I run along the water. But I dodge the trash talk, cutting to the chase. "Listen, you said something about the off-season and dating the woman I met then. Were you serious? Do you think it's a good idea?"

His expression turns deadly serious, his eyes like lasers. "Yeah, I was. But you didn't think it'd work. Did you change your tune?"

"Yes," I say, but that feels like a huge commitment and instantly I hedge my bets. "I mean, I think so."

He laughs, shaking his head. "Which one is it, buddy?"

I swallow, trying to sort out the feelings that are getting more tangled the longer I spend time with Brooke. "I'm thinking about it. If it'll work with her. What I need to do to *make it* work."

"If I learned anything from what Jason and Beck went through," he says, referring to his team's quar-

terback, who fell for the rival quarterback in San
Francisco, "it's that you need to figure out what you're
willing to gamble to get what you want."

That's the big question. What do I stand to gain?
What do I stand to lose? And what do I want? But I
think I already know the answer to the last one. "And
what if the answer is her? I want her."

"Damn, you really like her," he says with a
whistle.

"I do. It hasn't even been that long."

"When you know, you know," he says then we
end the call.

But will others accept the possibility of an *us* so
easily? Will Patrick, given what he knows about my
past relationships? Will Stephen? Will my new team?
I've only been with the Mercenaries a few weeks. I
don't want to rock the boat when I have this big
chance to show what I'm made of.

I'm also not sure if she'd want to give *us* a shot,
whatever *us* might be. Last week, she was noncommittal. She said being together in the off-season was
something to think about. But maybe she needs to
know I'm serious, that even though we started with a
one-night stand, I'm so ready for more than that.

But for the rest of the week I need to focus on the
Mercenaries, from the charity appearance Stephen
planned for me at a local library to an interview with
a sports blog.

And, of course, what happens on the field.

My team deserves my full attention. And that's what I give it, even as Carter's advice repeats in my mind.

* * *

When I run onto the field that Sunday, I savor the smell of the grass, the thunder of the crowd, and the rush of adrenaline pumping through my blood. In the huddle, I'm all business, and the Mercenaries are crisp.

We strike fast when I throw a twenty-yarder to Clements. He gives it a good home in his welcoming arms, then rushes for twenty more yards before he scrambles out of bounds.

Like that, we set a relentless pace, driving down-field until our running back puts us in the end zone.

Look at that. Two minutes into the game, and we've got seven points on the board. I rip off my helmet when I reach the sidelines, high-fiving Clements, then Rand, our running back.

Clements darts under the bench for his hacky sack, and then points at Rand. "You in or out? Adams and I have this thing—"

Rand scoffs. "I know. I'm fucking in."

The three of us kick the hacky sack during the commercial timeout, but game play resumes, and we give our attention to our brothers on D. We root on the defense as they force a fourth down from the Las

Vegas Pioneers. Then we're back on offense, and we put the ball in the end zone once again.

By halftime, we're up by twenty-one points, and Coach fights off a smile as he tells us to keep it up. Which we do, winning the game.

"Talk about a fucking streak," Clements shouts when I enter the locker room after the game.

I hold my arms out wide. "All I do is throw 'em. You're the one who catches 'em." I point to the guys on D. "And you all are an impenetrable wall."

The high spirits continue as I shower and dress. When I leave the locker room, Stephen's waiting for me in the corridor. "Stop making us look so smart for trading for you," he deadpans.

"Sorry, not sorry," I say.

He sighs contentedly. "Exactly." Then he shifts to business. "Tavarez called me over the weekend. Young Athletes has a fundraiser in a couple of weeks. Don't want to wear you out, but your name has come up as an emcee for the auction of sports memorabilia. Think about it. I know you're busy and—"

"I'm there," I say, cutting in with my yes.

"Stop making my job so easy," he says with a smile.

"Seriously, I'm happy to do it. And I got your message about the game night for the Every Kid organization on Tuesday. You can't keep me away from Skee-Ball."

"Terrific. I'll be there, and Brooke will stop by

too," he says. "And we've got a dinner Wednesday night—the three of us. To discuss all these upcoming events."

I hide a private grin at the bonus chances to see her this week and head to the exit to find Mom and the doubles. As I walk, though, a nagging voice dogs my heels.

You don't want to sneak a chance to see her. You want to see her for real.

But is she ready for that too? Is she even ready to talk about it? Or is it too soon to try to pull that off?

I grab my phone to fire off a text to Brooke, just to see if she enjoyed the game. And maybe to let her know I'm thinking about her. But I stop when I see Mom, Tom and the twins waiting for me at the door. I tuck my phone away. Now's not the time to be thinking about my secret affairs.

I try to stay in the moment as I take the family out for a late dinner at a trendy diner a few miles away.

"All right, got any game tips?" I ask Mom after we order.

"You're four for four. What could I possibly have to say?" she asks as Sophie grabs a pack of sugar.

"You must have something," I push.

"Don't throw a pick," Sophie says, as if she's

parroting someone. She's mainly busy setting a sugar packet on the end of her spoon.

Tom tsks, setting a gentle hand on hers. "Don't fling sugar. Not unless you're sure you can land it in a cup of water."

Sophie giggles.

Wide-eyed, I watch the exchange and then stare at Mom. "Were you praying against interceptions again?"

"What? I have my rituals too. I pray you won't throw picks."

"Don't get sacked. Don't get sacked," Mira says, with a devilish glint in her eyes, parroting Mom too.

Mom hides her face in her hand for a moment, then looks up, admitting, "Fine, the jig is up. I pray for good plays. And I pray against bad plays."

Reaching across the table, I ruffle her hair. "You're the cutest worrier," I say just as Tom snaps a pic of the moment.

"Sending to you now," he says to me. "It's so sweet. You should post that."

I love my mom, and I'm not posting it for cred. I'm posting it because she's the reason I can play ball for a living.

I caption it *My first coach and my biggest fan.*

I've relied on Mom for advice my whole life. When we're done eating, I let Tom and my sisters walk ahead of us, hanging back to snag a minute with her. "Need your advice, Mom."

"Of course. What is it?"

"There's this woman," I begin. I tell her most of the story—the PG version, that is. "So...what should I do?"

With a thoughtful smile, she says, "Well, have you told her how you feel? That might be a good way to start."

I stop walking. Stare at her.

Damn.

She's right.

She's so stinking right.

Maybe Brooke was noncommittal because I haven't put my heart on the line. Now that I've realized that, I want to tell her right now. Run to her house. Wake her up if she's sleeping.

Okay, maybe tonight isn't the time to do it. But I at least want to chat with her. To hear her voice. To keep sharing our days with each other.

When I get home, I click open my texts and find a message from her there waiting.

Brooke: You melted all the hearts in Los Angeles tonight with that post of you and your mom. And mine a little more.

I'd been looking for a sign. This seems crystal clear. I take a deep breath, open my emotions a little more.

Drew: Yours is the one I want.

Screw texts. I call her.

"Hey, honey," I say when she answers. That term of endearment feels different, as if it has new weight and meaning. "I hear you're going to the game night this week."

"Your sources are correct."

I stare out the window at the Pacific, a fuzzy warmth in my chest. "Then in our parallel universe, it should be a date."

Maybe somehow in the real world too.

"It definitely should be," she says, but her tone sounds a little distant.

"You okay?"

"Getting a migraine. So I took a pill. I'll probably fall asleep while we're talking," she says, apologetic.

"I might put you to sleep even without a headache," I tease.

"Very doubtful."

"You want me to let you go?"

"No. I like hearing from you." She yawns now, sleepy.

"I won't keep you long. Were you in the suite tonight?"

"I was. I enjoyed every second of it," she says. "How was time with your mom after?"

"It was great. Wish you could have had dinner with us."

"That would have been nice," she says with a soft sigh.

"Maybe someday," I say with hope.

"Yeah?" Her pitch rises too.

I'm this close to saying *I'm falling for you*. But with her starting to fade, now isn't the time. "I should let you sleep."

"Night, Drew," she says.

"Night, Brooke," I say.

But when I end the call, I'm not tired. I'm amped up with thoughts of her, and us, and our deal.

The deal I need to make good on. I pace in front of the window, staring at the dark sky, thinking.

What makes Brooke tick in bed? Dirty words. They're guaranteed to get her out of her head.

That gives me an idea.

What I need is a sex hack.

17

THE PROOF IS IN THE
WHAC-A-MOLE

Drew

Silas taunts me ferociously on Tuesday at the High Score Arcade in Santa Monica. "Prepare to lose once again, Drew!"

The seventh grade baseball player I've been battling in Whac-A-Mole is a tough competitor.

"Don't count me out yet." I lift the mallet and send a wooden mole into oblivion.

"Nope. You can't catch up," Silas says fiercely as I chase the vicious little moles in the game.

The tenacious kid has soundly whipped my ass in every game of Whac-A-Mole tonight. His baseball team was a rag tag bunch of middle schoolers with old equipment playing on overgrown fields until the

Mercenaries helped out through Every Kid, an organization that helps fund sports for underprivileged youth.

As my round ends in another loss, I lift my hand. "Silas, you are the king of Whac-A-Mole," I say, knocking fists with the young warrior. "Feel free to brag to all your teammates that you kicked my butt at Whac-A-Mole. Can you do that, my man?"

He beams. "I can do that. Can you win again this weekend against the San Francisco Hawks?"

I laugh, then clap him on the shoulder. "I'll do my best."

He heads off to join his buddies, and I return to the arcade game for a quick solo round.

As I clobber a mole, someone says in a pretty and familiar voice, "Carcful. I hear we might ban Whac-A-Mole next."

Slamming the padded hammer down on the wooden weasel, I answer with a grin. "The GM runs a tight ship," I say as the next mole submits to my speed with the hammer.

"But Skee-Ball is still safe," Brooke says.

"Whew. I was worried," I say, then sneak a glance at her.

Damn. Brooke is so pretty. Her tight red dress hits above her knees, and she looks good enough to eat.

All I want to do is kiss her. Go home with her. Take her out to breakfast and make her mine.

And just like that, I know tonight's the night to tell her.

A dopey grin spreads on my face. The moles pop up and I don't bother to hit them.

"I thought you were a Whac-A-Mole pro," she teases as she eyes the game board.

"I was." I dart my gaze around the arcade and drop my voice. "Then you walked over, looking like all my dirty dreams." But she's so much more than my bedroom fantasies. Gazing into her pretty brown eyes, I add, "And my daydreams."

Her breath catches. "Same for you," she whispers.

My body says *kiss her*. My heart says to do that too.

The way I feel for her can't be wrong. It blots out everything—the game, the rules, the team's image. It erases all the reasons I need to be cautious.

I inch toward her, and her eyes widen to saucer size. I freeze as she raises her chin, and mouths, *"Smile for the camera."*

In a split second, I turn and flash a grin at the photographer. Brooke smiles too, and the guy gives us a thumbs-up before he heads off to another group.

"Whew," she says. "That was close. I'm pretty sure you were trying to kiss me."

She doesn't sound mad.

She sounds...enchanted.

"I shouldn't have. But honey," I say, meeting her soft gaze, "I've got it bad for you."

Her smile is radiant, full of passion and possibility. "Drew," she says softly.

"And I really want to find a way for us."

"A way to what?" she asks, that cautious side of her in full swing.

"You and me," I mouth.

"You do want that?" she asks, hopeful.

"I do." I'm about to dive in, right there, and discuss what it'll take—when Stephen swoops in and shakes my hand. "Great night. Great event. Couldn't be more pleased. You?"

I nod. "Everything is fantastic."

The older man glances from Brooke to me and back. Something inquisitive passes through his eyes, and I feel a flurry of nerves, like when I can't find a receiver and I'm about to get sacked.

Maybe I was getting ahead of myself with my feelings' confession.

But Stephen's tone is relaxed as he says, "There's a soccer player who's keen for a round of Skee-Ball with the quarterback. She's eight and very competitive."

"It is on," I say, then head to the Skee-Ball games.

A serious blonde in a soccer jersey hands me a ball. "You go first," Phoebe says with a tone loaded with gravitas.

"Nope. Ladies first," I say, and with a small smile, Phoebe agrees, taking the ball.

"I've been practicing. I go after soccer games. If I don't become a pro soccer player, I'm going to play Skee-Ball."

"Those are some excellent goals," I say.

We play a few rounds, and I do my best to keep it fair. But it's hard to check my competitive nature at the door.

Then, I play a round with Brooke, and I clobber her. That's kind of weirdly satisfying. But afterward, she gestures to the exit. "I have a late call with a supplier I need to take from home. But it was good to see you," she says, and briefly a look passes between us—one that says *it was so good to see you tonight*.

When she leaves, I watch her go longer than I should. As my gaze lingers, Stephen returns to me with the head of Every Kid.

We chat for a while about some of the work his organization has done to expand sports access, and when we're done, Stephen pulls me aside.

"We have a press tour coming up to show some of the bloggers and podcasters around the stadium—those who don't usually come in person to cover the games. We're showcasing the new food booths, do a tour, then some photos. Any chance you'd want to join in? It'd be great to see you there," he says, ending on an upbeat tone.

My calendar is getting full, but I should be able to fit in a tour and some pics. Besides, it's the right thing to do, especially with the way the Mercenaries are treating me.

"Absolutely," I say.

I play a few more rounds with the kids, and soon, the stars are winking in the sky.

When the event winds down, I find my phone blinking with a note.

Brooke: Want to come over? I made this.

There's a mouthwatering photo of chicken and cauliflower drizzled in cheese, with brussels sprouts on the side, and I want to lick the phone.

Drew: Your food porn worked. The answer is yes. But where's the pic of your legs?

Brooke: I knew the food porn would be enough to lure you here.

Drew: You were wrong. I'm coming for you. But also, the food.

Brooke: I was right.

I grab a Lyft and go, ready to try my sex hack and perhaps devise a romance one too.

18

HIS SEX HACK

Brooke

My call was over in all of five minutes, so I used the unexpected free time to whip up a quick dish, then Rachel stopped by on her way home from work.

She lives a few blocks away, and I've caught her up on all the man things in my life.

Now, she cinches a necklace at the back of my neck. "There," she says as I let my hair fall and then spin around to face her in the kitchen. "So cute. Do you like it, Brooke?"

As the cauliflower dish cools, I peer in the camera on my phone, admiring the sparkly chain with the silver charm—three little books stacked together. She saved it for me when it arrived at her nearby boutique earlier today.

"It's fantastic," I say, but it reminds me of Drew, and my stomach swoops with unexpected nerves.

Or maybe this feeling is expected, knowing Drew will be here soon.

I set a hand on my belly.

She eyes me curiously. "You okay?"

"Just feeling…I dunno. Vulnerable?"

"If you decide not to tell him how you feel tonight, that's fine too." She squeezes my arm. "Do it in your time, okay?"

I'm such a worrier. So risk averse. "It's too soon, right?" I squeak. Am I ready to brave the *I'm falling for you* conversation?

"Brooke, who am I to decide how soon it is? Feelings are feelings," she says. "You figure them out in your own time. Not anyone else's."

"But especially after Sailor." I fiddle with a dish towel. "Maybe it's too soon to trust someone else."

Even though Sailor and I split nearly a year ago.

Rachel shakes her head emphatically, her chestnut hair flying. "Just because your ex was a cheater doesn't mean a damn thing about this guy."

I finger the charm. "It's all a lot easier in books."

"Maybe," she says with a sympathetic smile. "But sometimes you just want to live your own story, you know?"

What if it's not about the timing? Maybe I'm the obstacle, my own worries, my mistrust, my fear of getting hurt again holding me back. Yes, Drew and I have our challenges. Is the biggest one...me?

"Ugh. Stop being wise." I shoo her out with a potholder and shut the door. Then I rest against it, thinking over the last few weeks of getting to know Drew.

Something deep and true is happening between us.

He said as much tonight. I've been feeling it too. Which seems wild and risky, but also, it's so real.

I return to the kitchen, checking on the chicken dish as it cools. After I set out utensils and napkins, I settle in at the counter and dive back into my new book, a romance novel that Rachel turned me onto —*Top-Notch Boyfriend*. The opening hooked me, and I'm eager to dive back in.

But I can't stay focused on the pages. Even though books have always been my escape, I can't seem to run from this drumbeat in my heart. It's loud and insistent, telling me to ask for what I want.

It's telling me to take a chance.

To ride the wave.

To put myself out there.

Seconds later, the doorbell rings, and I race to the door, ready to blurt out, *I want to try.*

But Drew's faster. "Bed. Now. I'm making good on our deal right fucking now, then the next night and the next and the next."

I blink, then just rasp out a *yes*.

* * *

My normal sex worries swim up once I'm on my back on the bed, but not like they used to. Not as loud. Not as annoying.

"I've got you tonight," Drew whispers as he climbs over me, his voice smoky as he smothers my neck in kisses. My neck is his playground, and he covers it in caresses, gentle kisses, then hungrier nips.

When he presses his lips to the hollow of my throat, my stomach flips. Then he moves down my body, pushes up my skirt, and pulls down my panties.

He groans in appreciation, then he moves back up me, grabs his phone from the mattress and his earbuds too. "I've got a sex hack for you. Put these on. I know you like dirty talk, and my mouth is about to be occupied with your sweet pussy."

It takes a beat to register what he's done, but then I get it. I smile wickedly as I pop in the earbuds.

A few seconds later, he's talking to me in my ears as he moves down my body.

Oh.

Wow.

That feels so good.

Then it's even better when the recording he made of his own sexy voice plays.

You're so slick and wet. You taste so fucking sweet.

He kisses me.

Rock those hips against my face.

I obey, arching into him. He kisses me ravenously, licking sensual lines up and down.

I fucking love burying my face between your thighs.

The pleasure sharpens as he spreads my legs wide, kissing me deeply, passionately.

I want to make your legs shake, your knees weak. Want you to tremble as I kiss you between your legs and fuck you with my tongue.

I moan from his words, from his touch, from his hands, from his mouth. The erotic overload drowns out my worries, replacing them with pure lust and joy as I arch against him, running my fingers through his hair.

I've gotten off to this so many times. I jack off to you in the shower.

Sharp, hot pleasure thrums through me.

Want you to come on my face.

I want that too. So badly. I'm so close.

Fuck, honey. You taste so fucking good.

Pressing his hands on my thighs, he spreads my legs wider, then drapes them over his shoulders.

Gripping the strands of his hair harder, I tug him closer still. My belly tightens, and I near the edge.

Then, I'm chanting *oh God, oh God, oh God* over

and over as I rock my hips into his face, curl my hands tight around his head, and shatter beautifully.

I come undone on his lips in a wild frenzy.

He figured me out. He cracked the code with his sex hack, and I feel so damn good about the chance I want to take with him.

19

THE GLOAT

Drew

I'm feeling pretty cocky as I devour the food porn. I laugh, shaking my head with each bite of the cheesy chicken and cauliflower.

"What is it?" she asks.

I wiggle a brow. "Just thinking that I made you come hard."

"And that makes you gloat?"

"Fuck yes," I say, then I dive in for a kiss. "I thought about our deal *a lot*. I wanted to give you what I'd promised. And it helps that I think about you naked pretty much all the time."

"Were you thinking about me naked at the Skee-Ball machine?" she asks as she takes a forkful of the dish.

I laugh. "Oh yes. I saw you, and I undressed you mentally. Hope you don't object," I say.

She dips her face, shaking her head.

She clearly enjoys the sexy compliments, but I don't want to dwell in sexy land. "You know I want more than the sex," I say, setting down my fork. "I want to give you a kiss when you show up at the Whac-A-Mole game. Put my arm around you in between Skee-Ball rounds. Take your hand in mine as we leave together." I hold her gaze and tell her, "I don't want to sneak around, Brooke."

Her brown eyes sparkle, emboldening me to go on. To share my heart. God, I hope she returns these feelings. "I was going to ask if we could make a go of things in the off-season, but—fuck it. I want you now. I'll do whatever it takes for us to make things work. Do you want to?"

"I do, but I worry too," she says, fingering her necklace.

"I know you do." I'm the gambler between the pair of us. I take chances for a living. I can lend her some of my faith and confidence. "Would it really be such a bad thing if we were together? I thought so at first, wondering how it would look if anyone found out I come over here at night. But we're not just messing around anymore."

"We're not," she says, emphatic.

Yes. Fucking *yes.*

"And that's why I don't think the player and the

executive is such a bad look after all. I'm just a twenty-eight-year-old guy who's got his shit together and wants to go out with a woman he works with—a woman who has her act together too," I say, taking her hand.

"Imagine if the press found out I—gasp—am teaching you to cook?"

"Or if they heard we saw a cute sports flick together?" I say drily.

"And how about that time"—she goes full-cringe —"we went for a walk?"

"The paps would have a field day, especially over the chicken and cauliflower."

She threads her fingers through mine, grinning confidently now too. That fuels me, pushes me on to seal my case.

"The team is strong. We've played like rock stars, and this secret thing hasn't hurt me on the field at all so far this season." I can't mask the hope in my voice. "Plus, did you see how Stephen looked at you, then at me tonight? It was almost like he was pleased to see us together."

Her mouth curves in a conspiratorial grin. "He seemed intrigued. Curious." She licks her lips and shrugs happily. "I don't know what's next. But I want to try with you."

I pop up from the stool, cup her cheek, and kiss her.

Then, we make a plan. She'll feel him out at

work. We're supposed to have dinner with him at a new restaurant in Venice tomorrow night. We'll tell him then, together.

Then, my gaze drifts down to her necklace again. That's new. I touch the book charm. "Where'd you get this?"

"My friend Rachel brought it over for me. She owns a jewelry shop and thought of me when it came into her store. "

"Because you love to read," I say.

"Yes, but it also reminded me of the day I met you."

"When you were doing one of your favorite activities," I say, smiling.

"Yup. But let's do another one of my favorite activities now."

I toss her over my shoulder and carry her to the bedroom.

20

HOW TO SAY MASTERMIND

Brooke

As I park in the stadium lot in the morning, Cara's name blinks on my phone.

I answer right away, jumping at the chance to poke fun at my hearts-and-flowers sister. "Are you calling to tell me about your latest *amazing* date with Patrick?"

She's been seeing him since the night at the movies, and everything is *the best*. "Gah. Yes. He's so sweet," she says, then tells me about the game of mini golf they played last night. And mini golf isn't even a euphemism.

"I haven't heard you like this about a guy in, well, ever," I say.

"He's funny and smart, and he's kind of smitten too."

Cara deserves a good guy. Her college boyfriend was a leading candidate for Toxic Love. He smothered her, constantly calling and texting, showing up unannounced—in short, stalking her.

"So Patrick's attentive, but not too much?" I ask carefully.

"Just the right amount. I swear," she says. "He gives me space when I need it, and he's around when I want him to be."

"Good. I'm glad. I worry about you," I say as I pull open the door to the front office.

She snorts. "Understatement of the year."

I bristle. "I'm allowed to worry about my baby sister."

"And I appreciate it, but I swear everything is good. Now...what about you and Drew? I haven't said anything to Patrick about you two..." But the way she trails off makes it sound like she wants to.

"Good," I say, then take a deep breath. "But maybe soon it won't have to be secret."

Wow, that felt strange to say, and a little uncomfortable, but only because I'm getting used to the idea of *not* hiding.

I hope.

"Really? Are you guys going to do this for real?"

"We've talked about it," I say softly, floating the

idea out loud since I'll have to float it to Stephen any second now.

"What are you going to do?"

I'm flying blind here, but I've given it a lot of thought in the last twenty-four hours. "I want to talk to my boss. Try to understand what's possible. I know how to ask things without implicating myself or Drew."

"I'm rooting for you," she says, her enthusiasm loud and clear.

I thank her, then say goodbye and head inside. Once I reach my office, I settle in with the employee handbook, digging into any guidelines on employee-player relationships. There's not much in here—the only guideline is that dating a co-worker should be disclosed to human resources.

I'll start with my boss.

I take a deep, fueling breath, push back in my chair, and stand up so I can find Stephen.

Only, there's no need to track him down. The tall, shrewd man is knocking on my open door. My stomach dips. I'm hardly ready. Do I say, *Hey, what would you think if I dated the quarterback?* Or maybe, *Stephen, I have a funny story to tell you involving a paddle board oar, a margarita, and me.*

"Come in," I say instead.

He closes the door behind him and chooses the chair across from my desk. "About last night…"

I sit up straighter, nerves tightening. "The Every Kid event?"

Did he overhear our sweet nothings at Whac-A-Mole? Cold fear seeps into my bones. Just because I was about to march into his office for a heart-to-heart doesn't mean he'll rubber stamp my plan.

My messy, unformed plan.

What the hell is my plan, anyway?

All my clarity slinks out the door. I need this job. I have loans to pay off. Drew needs to have a good season. The team is rehabbing its image.

What am I doing?

"You and Adams," Stephen adds.

A weight lodges in my chest. Keeping a blank face, I wait for him to say more.

Stephen clears his throat. "Did I pick up on a vibe?"

"What vibe do you mean?" I ask evenly.

He spins his phone around, slides his thumb across the screen.

My body is a high-tension line as he shows me a photo from last night on a sports gossip site. The shot is of Drew and me talking by the Whac-A-Mole.

Flirting, really.

But the caption reads: *Mercenaries QB playing a boardwalk game with the team's attorney.*

Like the site thinks we're cute?

Stephen's gray eyes flicker with Machiavellian delight. "Fun pic, right?" He swipes the screen again and displays another. "Just like this one the reporter found."

He shows me a picture I've seen before—the one taken at the first event at the hotel, in front of the Young Athletes banner for the charity. *Here they are last month at the Young Athletes event. Hmmm* ☺

"And that gave you a vibe?" I ask, stripping emotion from my voice until I'm sure what he's after.

"A vibe and an idea," he says. "Especially when I came across this shot." He hands me the phone once more. I gulp. The picture of the four of us leaving *Fake Play* is new to me. Looks like it was taken from a distance. Was a photographer stalking Drew that night?

The caption reads *QB and friends seeing fake romance movie.*

"Where's that from?" I ask, wildly curious.

Stephen shrugs. "Just some fan. Someone was eating at Ruby's Taco Truck, then posted this shot of you guys too," he says, like those details don't interest him.

It seems Stephen's not interpreting the handbook the same way I am, and his interpretation is the one that matters.

"We ran into each other. I was with my sister, and he was with his friend, so we all saw the movie together," I explain, feeling like I've been called into the principal's office.

And I'm doing a horrible job telling Stephen I

want to date Drew. I'm backpedaling. I'm *untelling* him.

I am the worst.

He waves a hand dismissively. "That's all fine. The fake romance movie and the pics got me thinking. You two seemed like a real couple. And I thought, wouldn't it be great if they *were* together? This happy couple on the team. Maybe even going to dinner tonight in Venice Beach."

Ohhhhh.

Is he saying what I think he's saying?

"I thought we were having dinner with you tonight?" I want to be crystal clear on his meaning.

"You can take my reservation. Just the two of you. Let me be blunt, Brooke." He clasps his hands together. "With all the shit this team went through last year, this potential love affair is looking to be a bright spot—the quarterback playing Skee-Ball with kids, and then with the woman he likes at a charity function. An upstanding, respected attorney. What a delightful story. Co-workers falling for each other. It made me think if I were writing a movie script, I'd craft this kind of romance because the press is eating it up."

Oh, my stars. That's why he sounds so...delightfully calculated. He wants me to date Drew? Or wait. Does he want me to fake date him? "So you want me to pretend date him? Or date him for real?"

Stephen smiles devilishly. "What a great idea you

just had." He drops his voice to a whisper. "But make it seem real."

But it is *real.*

I try to make those words pass my lips, but he heads for the door, checking his watch. "I've got a call. The reservation is at eight under my name, and I'll adjust it for two. Look natural if someone takes your pic. There's little the public loves more than when the squeaky-clean quarterback wins the heart of a good woman, so carry on. There's even that press tour next week of the new food booths here at the stadium. He'll be there. You'll be there. I'll make sure HR knows, so everything's on the up and up," he says as he walks away, dropping the mic and leaving me to fake-date the quarterback with his blessing.

Or real date?

I don't even know which one. Or if it matters. But I know this—I'm expected to be seen with him tonight at eight.

I sink into the chair, shell-shocked, trying to figure out how in the hell that happened. Then I open my phone to send Drew a text.

Brooke: So, this is an unexpected twist. Stephen got a vibe from us, he said. He wants us to be fake dating. Or maybe he thinks we're real dating. It doesn't matter. I was so shocked when he told me he thinks

we're adorable together and that it'd be a great idea if
we *were* together.

Drew: Holy fuck, that's all that matters, honey!
Because we are.

Brooke: This is so surreal. He even changed the
dinner reservation this evening so it's just for two.

Drew: Except it's the real world, finally. We're not in
the parallel one any longer, and tonight, I'm taking
you out.

I guess I didn't screw this up. At least I don't think so.

21

BE CAREFUL WHAT YOU WISH FOR

Brooke

"Can I interest you in wine?"

It's a simple enough question from the server at Max's, but I draw a blank.

I glance at Drew, then at the goateed server, then back at Drew. Am I supposed to order liquor? Is that acceptable for a fake date? A fake real date? Should I order lemonade instead?

I'm...flummoxed

Drew lifts a brow. "You like chardonnay usually, right, honey?"

He must think I've spaced out.

But if I order wine, will that make me sound like a lush in the sports press? Is the media going to say I have a drinking problem?

"I'll have a Perrier," I choke out.

"And for you, sir?" the man asks Drew.

"Same," he says with a smile, so natural when I'm so not.

When the guy leaves, Drew shoots me a curious look. "You okay, Brooke?"

"I'm great," I chirp.

But do I look annoyed? Wait. Do I look appropriate? I'm wearing a red blouse and jeans. Is that proper fake dating attire? Should I have worn a boho dress? A cute little hat? A slouchy top?

Where is the handbook for this, Stephen?

"How was your day?" I ask Drew, pasting on a smile. Like we always have cheery, PR-y, media-friendly conversations. Not like we play with innuendos, talk dirty, share stories, or chat about hopes and dreams and orgasms.

"It was good. Worked out, ran with Patrick, practiced. I told Patrick about us," he says, his shoulders relaxed, his eyes bright.

He's happy and relieved.

But I can't shake the sense someone is watching. Probably because someone, somewhere, *is*.

"You did?" I glance around. Someone is probably listening too.

What if some fan finds out how long our fling has been going on? A reporter? A blogger? Will we be *sooo cute* then?

"How did it go?" I ask.

Drew takes a few seconds before he answers, like he's weighing something—or maybe editing himself? I can't quite tell. Then he smiles and says, "He got a kick out of learning you're my taco-spank-ings woman."

"Shhh," I hiss.

Shoot. Did I just sound like a shrew? Disciplining my boyfriend? Wait. Is he my boyfriend?

My stomach churns.

"My bad," Drew says, chastened.

My heart slams against my chest. I feel so foolish. "It's fine."

"He's happy for us. He's a good guy, like I told you, and he understood why I kept it quiet. But he said for the rest of time, he will look for a chance to pretend he's you via text."

I laugh, but it fades quickly.

Drew stretches a hand across the table. "But seriously, are you okay?"

I peer around. Is that skinny guy at the bar going to take our picture? The woman with the pierced nose? The couple taking selfies?

"I'm fine," I lie.

Pretending to real date him is harder than sneaking around.

* * *

I wake the next morning to a slew of pics of us on social—laughing at Max's, toasting with Perrier, eating scallops.

We're apparently the new *it* couple.

Quarterback Drew Adams and his new GF Brooke Holland, an attorney for the team, were spotted dining at Max's in Venice last night. Aww, they're like an office romance! I wonder where they had their meet-cute? Outside the locker room? Or did the QB stop by the break room to make a cup of Joe? We want to know!

What would they say if they knew we met on the beach over a month ago? Sneaked around a few times? That he got me off in traffic?

My stomach swoops as I walk into work.

Felipe gives me a thumbs-up.

Nancy catcalls with a *you go, girl*.

At least they aren't talking about Sailor and how hot my ex is.

Until I walk past Abby's desk in analytics. "You have the hottest exes," she says, then stammers, "I-I mean boyfriends. The hottest boyfriends."

They're not *both* my boyfriends. But I don't correct her. I smile, like I'm doing a toothpaste commercial. Then I shut my door, blow out a breath, and dive into work.

When Stephen stops by, he looks more relaxed than I've seen him in ages. "I trust Max's was good."

"Fantastic," I say brightly. I don't want to sound ungrateful. It's not easy to snag a table there. Besides, he doesn't want to hear how exhausting it is to fake it, yet not fake it.

"Last night looked great. Maybe take a walk along the beach some evening," he says, like a conductor of this fake real boyfriend theater.

Code for *do it tonight.*

I want to just be alone with Drew. But Drew is the face of the franchise, and Drew draws fans, and Drew is great in public.

Really, I can't complain that I'm going for a walk with the guy I've been secretly longing to publicly date.

* * *

That night, we stroll along the sandy shores of Venice Beach. Do I hold his hand? Put an arm around his waist?

When he comes in to kiss my lips, I dart away, giving him the cheek.

"Brooke, I can tell you're uncomfortable," he says, his brow creased. "What can I do?"

I can't stand feeling so tense, so wound up. "It's just weird. I feel like I can't be myself. I've always felt like myself with you—until now."

As soon as I say it, I want to kick myself for complaining.

I wanted this, right?

I wanted to be with him for real.

But I don't want to do it wrong. I don't know how to do it *right* as a public couple.

"You didn't feel like yourself last night either, did you?"

He knows me so well already. I'm grateful, though, that he gets me. That he sees the issue.

"No," I answer. "I just wanted to tease you and make innuendos, and play footsie, and kiss you at the table, and..." All at once, my tension loosens into a sex confession.

"Climb me in public?" he murmurs with a lascivious raise of his brows.

"Kind of," I admit, then I spill more of my concerns. "Are we supposed to be a nice guy/nice girl couple? Because I'm not. I want you to—"

He shuts me up with a kiss.

A very un-chaste kiss, very much in public.

When we break it, I say, "I want you to take me home and fuck me."

It's the first thing that's felt real since this fake dating started.

* * *

He parks himself on my couch and pats his legs. "Get on me and ride me."

Hell yes. He's not using a condom. We're both negative and exclusive, so I straddle him, and he grasps my hips, positioning me over his cock.

I ease down, his strong hands digging into my hips as he guides me. I lean in closer, my breasts brushing his chest.

"Just you and me now," he murmurs. "Use my dick to get off, honey."

I shudder from the pleasure rushing through me already. "I love riding your cock."

His eyes darken. His growl deepens. "That's right. Use my dick to get off, and use this beautiful mouth too," he says, running a finger along my bottom lip. "Love it when you say filthy things."

"Love it when you fuck me hard," I counter as he thrusts, stroking up.

His big hands run along my waist until he covers my belly with one palm. There's something deliciously possessive in the gesture.

"You look so fucking beautiful riding my cock, Brooke." His voice is a filthy whisper, but tender somehow too.

I moan, letting my head fall back as I find my perfect pace, rocking up and down on him.

"Love the way your sweet pussy grips me," he rasps out, and I gasp at the lovely smut.

We become a hot, wild thing, a smashing of sweaty, greedy bodies. I'm nothing but desire and the wish to come. As my muscles tense, pleasure erupts everywhere inside me.

Seconds later, he follows me, pounding me hard,

rough, like the lashing of rain against a window as he joins me.

Soon, we collapse in a sweaty heap on my couch, and he smothers my neck in kisses, then my cheek, then my ear. "Hey, you."

"Hey, you."

"I'm falling for you," he says.

I smile. "I'm falling so hard for you."

22

A CLEAN SHAVE

Drew

Best week ever.

I've spent every evening at Brooke's home except last night, when she slept here with me at my condo. After a fantastic round of morning sex, I walk her to the door on Saturday and give her a long, lingering kiss goodbye. "See you on Monday," I say.

"See you then," she says, then breezes out.

The team flies to San Francisco tomorrow morning for a Sunday night game against Carter's local rivals—the San Francisco Hawks. I hurry to get ready to head to the stadium for a review of the playbook before tomorrow's kickoff.

But when I open the door to leave, I stop short.

Patrick stands outside, his fist poised to knock.

"Hey man, what's up?" I ask, my brow furrowed. "I need to head to the stadium."

"Just this little thing known as a meeting." He taps his watch. "I was at the coffee shop down the block with Tavarez, waiting for you. To talk about the donations you're making, the role he wants you to play. Pretty sure he wants you on the board. But you didn't show. What's up?"

Oh, shit.

I'm a dick.

"I'm sorry." I drag a hand through my hair. "I totally forgot."

He gives me a quizzical look. "That's not like you. But that's why I texted to see what was up. I called too. You didn't get either?"

"Um," I say, rubbing a hand across the back of my neck. Truth was, I was busy with Brooke all morning. My face between her thighs and all. Didn't check my phone. Didn't even turn it on. "Must have missed it. I'm sorry. I feel like a jerk."

Patrick's a chill dude, and rarely gets ruffled. But he's clearly concerned. "You getting enough sleep?" His protective side is out in full force. "You've always needed a solid eight hours."

I do the math. I've been nowhere close to that. More like six, maybe seven. But the sex and the conversations with Brooke are so worth it. "I'm close to that."

"Good. I'm guessing you missed my message this morning because you were busy with your woman?"

It doesn't sound like a reprimand. More like a *hey, I'm looking out for you.* I feel like a jackass, though.

"Is he still there? I can meet with him now."

"He had to take off. Something with his kid. But we'll reschedule. It happens," Patrick says.

But it doesn't happen to me. I don't miss meetings. I don't forget obligations. My mom taught me to show up, and I motherfucking do.

Maybe I have sex brain.

"I'll do better next week. I promise," I say.

Patrick claps me on the shoulder. "No worries. Glad you're into her, man. Just keep your focus."

He leaves, and before I take off for work, I send Paul a message apologizing for my no-show and telling him I can't wait to talk to him about Young Athletes.

At the stadium, we review the game plan, and I put both the missed meeting and the woman out of my mind. I have tunnel vision the rest of the day and into Sunday morning as we board the plane for the hour-long flight. By the time we hit the Hawks field for kickoff, I'm in the zone.

* * *

We score first. But the Hawks are tough as nails. Their quarterback is fearless in the pocket and lasers in on his receivers on every damn throw.

The quarterback, Jason McKay, is a steely-eyed missile man, and he connects, matching the score.

But no biggie. I'll keep putting my guys ahead.

Except on the next play, when I take the snap and hunt for an open receiver, I find nada.

I tuck the ball under my arm, ready to scramble for a few yards, when out of nowhere, a Hawks linebacker slams me to the ground.

All the air evacuates my lungs.

My head rings.

And I wince as my left tackle offers me his hand, tugs me up. "You okay, man?"

"I'll be fine. Thanks," I say to Theo.

I try to shake off the sack, then I get back in the huddle. But on the next snap, I fire too early and send a pick right into Xavier Walters' arms. The Hawks cornerback returns it for a touchdown.

"Fuck me," I mutter as he celebrates in the end zone.

I walk off the field, head down. Clements pats my back.

"I brought a blue hacky sack today," he says, but I'm not in the mood to play games.

I shake him off, then when we get possession again, we're over and out in four. We punt, and I fail to move the ball the rest of the half.

Somehow, the second half is even worse. I throw another interception on our first drive. On our next possession, I'm sacked, and this might be the worst game of my life.

I cannot find a rhythm.

When the game mercifully ends, I feel beaten and bruised.

I trudge into the locker room, away from the scene of the pummeling. In front of his stall, Rand scrubs a hand over his smooth jaw.

"This is my fault," he says. "I was growing a beard, and my girlfriend said it was itchy, so I shaved and look what happened."

"Pretty sure it was my shitty throws, not your beard or no beard," I say.

Rand shakes his head adamantly. "No, man. You never fuck with a streak. It ruins your luck. And I did. I fucked with the football gods."

The conversation nags at me as I shower, as we fly home late that night.

Maybe you don't fuck with a streak.

But not for the reasons he said. Not because of luck, or superstition, or football gods shining in your favor when you grow a beard.

You don't fuck with a streak because it ruins your focus.

Focus in football is everything. The sport isn't just a physical game—it's a mental one. Quarterbacks who win need to blot out the world. They need to stay in the zone, and only in the zone.

Once inside my home, I flick on the TV and force of habit takes me straight to the Sports Network. I crank up the volume. The anchor launches into her football recap and, soon enough, lands on my team.

"Drew Adams has been playing impeccably, but today the Los Angeles Mercenaries earned their first L of the season in one of the worst games of his career. Let's dig into what broke their four-and-zero record."

Part of me wants to shout, "It was just four games."

But another, deeper part of me knows that every goddamn game matters. Muting the TV, I close my eyes, replaying the game from the start.

Where did I go wrong? The Mercenaries have played like a smooth, well-oiled machine for the last month.

Until...

I shudder at the thought.

But then I say it quietly aloud.

"Until I stopped focusing on football," I mutter.

The second I leveled up with Brooke, my game play fell apart in spectacular fashion.

Maybe I can't have romance and football. Maybe I need to choose one or the other.

No!

Stop that shit.

I'm not buying into that.

That's ridiculous.

Instead, I send Brooke a text so she knows I'm thinking of her. *Hey honey, I'm zonked. Going to bed. See you tomorrow.*

We meet the next morning for an early coffee on the Promenade before she goes into work. Patrick and Cara join us at an outdoor table at Big Cup Café.

"Tough loss," Patrick says with sympathy.

"I played horribly," I reply, still sullen.

"You didn't seem that focused," Patrick says without judgment. Just the awareness of someone who's seen most of my games.

Brooke tilts her head, listening. "You think that was the issue?" she asks, she's not quite buying what he's selling.

"It reminded me of your senior year," Patrick says. "When you had a few rough games that October."

I blink. Holy shit. Yesterday's game *did* feel a lot like those clunkers.

The painful memories crawl to the surface. Marie was an exchange student at college my senior year. I met her at a party at the start of the semester and was instantly taken. I started spending more time with her, seeing her on the reg.

"Just…" Patrick starts, then stops.

"What happened then?" Cara asks.

Patrick waves a hand, like he's covering it up. "Just a few bad games."

"And what was the reason, sweetie?" Cara asks Patrick, pushing harder for an answer from him.

Ah, hell. Poor Patrick's about to get a grilling from his woman. Over me. I need to tell them. Not him.

"I met someone. I was really into her. And I had a few bad games because she was all I could think about."

The confession is full of remembered embarrassment over how I played. Brooke frowns, but then she erases it, her face a tabula rasa.

"But it's not the same," I say quickly.

Except, what if this situation *is* the same? What if I can't balance football and romance?

"And you missed a meeting the other morning?" Brooke asks, reminding me of yet another fuckup this past week.

I look away, ashamed over that too. "Yeah, but I rescheduled with Paul, so it's all good."

Patrick clears his throat and points to the interior of the café. "I'm going to grab a coffee."

"Me too," Cara says.

Once they're inside, Brooke meets my gaze and says gently, "So there have been other times when you struggled to balance football and dating?"

I swallow uncomfortably. If I say yes, I'll sound like I don't have my shit together. But then, maybe I don't. I stay quiet.

"Senior year of college is an important time," she adds, her tone full of understanding. "With recruiting and the draft and such."

"That's true," I admit, recalling those terrible early season games and my worries that I was blowing my shot at the pros.

"And you probably stressed about whether it would affect your chances in the draft," she says, kind and thoughtful, getting me too well.

I look away, rubbing a hand along the back of my neck. "Yeah, I did."

"And did you break it off with her?" she asks, still soft and caring.

I wince but mumble a yes.

"And did your game improve?"

Grimacing, I bite out a yes again.

I hate that yes.

Hate it so fucking much.

She draws a deep breath then reaches for my hand, squeezing it. "Would it help if maybe we took a week off? Or perhaps more? I don't want this to get you down."

No! God, no. Not at all.

Except...what if I'm terrible at balancing every-thing? What if I lost my focus? What if I can't manage it all?

"I really don't want to," I say heavy and resigned because I probably should say yes. "But..."

She purses her lips. "But maybe it's for the best?"

I grimace. Damn, she has more guts than I do.

More insight too.

No way can this be the answer. Except the evidence adds up. I thought so last night, but I didn't want to put the clues together. Now, I don't know what else to think.

"Maybe it is best," I say, wishing that weren't the answer, but fearing it is. "But what about the media tour?"

"Drew," she says, her voice soft but her tone firm. "Maybe you're doing too much. You say yes to everything. You do all these charity events, which is amazing. You do all these interviews. But perhaps you're spreading yourself too thin. I can talk to Stephen, and we can find someone else. Another player. Maybe Clements."

My shoulders relax, and I hate that I want that so much. But I do. That would be a load off.

"You wouldn't mind?" I ask.

She shakes her head. "I'll take care of it. You just focus on football."

"And next week?" I'm hopeful I can see her again, but is that even fair to ask? Does that make me a fair-weather boyfriend?

No, I can't ask her to date again next week. I need to get my shit together before I can fully commit.

"Focus on this week," she says, echoing my thoughts, more caring than I deserve. "That's all you should concentrate on."

It sounds like a good plan. But it also sounds like we just put our romance on ice.

23

HIS BAD LUCK CHARM

Brooke

When I walk down the hall in the office an hour later, I get the sense that my co-workers are whispering about me again.

But not for long, since Felipe says out loud, "Did you make him feel better this morning?"

"What do you mean?" I ask, stopping at his desk.

"Well, there was that cute pic of you two having coffee a little while ago. You were holding his hand," he says, like Drew and I are the height of adorbs. He pops up from his desk, phone in hand, and swings it my way. A social media feed from *MercenaryFanGirl* features a shot of me holding Drew's hand this morning.

The back of my neck prickles. We were seen an

hour ago while we were, for all intents and purposes, breaking up.

Only this fan has no clue what really went down.

My stomach churns with the utter wrongness of the caption. *QB's GF comforts him after yesterday's tough loss.*

Yeah, some comfort I gave. More like I freed him from his obligation.

I was his albatross. His bad luck charm.

"Thanks for sharing," I say blandly to Felipe, then stare at my shoes as I walk to my office, hoping to avoid any more run-ins.

But when I pass Abby, she catches my attention with a "Psst," then asks, "How is he doing after yesterday?"

My throat tightens as I choke out, "Fine."

My door is ten feet away. If I can just make it past the moat of hungry co-workers who dine on gossip...

I'm almost past the threshold, when a familiar voice slithers up my spine.

"Morning, Brooke. I have a horchata."

Screw horchatas.

I spin to face him and slap on a grin. "Thanks. But I just had a coffee."

Stephen frowns. "Too bad. Maybe I'll drink it." He follows me into my office, taking a hearty swallow from one cup. "Damn, this is one fine drink."

Well, maybe the latte was for him all along.

"Anyway, I wanted to get this as a thanks," he

says, then shakes his head but in obvious approval. "You're nailing this *dating thing*." With his free hand, he sketches air quotes.

Probably because he doesn't want to say "fake dating" out loud.

Only it was never fake. And I'm a little tired of acting like maybe it was.

I'm tired of the charade.

And after this morning's heartbreak, I don't want to fake a thing anymore. Especially since I'll have to tell him in three seconds that it's over. I was hoping I'd have some more time to break the bad news.

"I'm glad to hear, but the thing is—"

"The Mercenaries are such a fan-favorite now, thanks to Drew. Sure, the sports news hammered the team yesterday with the loss to the Hawks, but social media is trending with how cute you are together. The fans are loving the two of you."

I can't deal with this anymore.

I close the door, meet his eyes, and say, "I hate to tell you this..."

After the botched job I did *untelling* him I was dating Drew, I've got to do it right now. "He's not coming to the press tour this week. He's got a lot on his plate, Stephen. He needs to focus on football. So we won't attend as a couple."

Stephen is rarely rattled.

But he's not simply rattled. He's speechless. His mouth hangs open unceremoniously. "You won't?"

"We won't." I swallow the stones in my throat, wishing I didn't have to say this. "And I don't know if we'll be able to attend any others."

My voice cracks. It's full of potholes I didn't see coming.

"Did you fake break up?" he asks, even more confused.

My shoulders shake. Tears prick the back of my eyes. Stupid tears. Foolish emotions. "Honestly, it was real. We were together for real, Stephen. And now we're not."

And there's nothing fake about the hurt in my heart right now.

24

RINSE, LATHER, REPEAT

Drew

Maddox would tell me not to listen, but on the drive to the stadium I stick my finger in the flame and tune in to Pigskin Jimbo, a nationally syndicated sports talk host.

There's nothing quite as sobering as a raspy-voiced dude lambasting you in front of millions of listeners for every single play.

"One of the sloppiest games I've ever watched. I watched it through my fingers, horror-movie style," he barks. "What do you think? Let's hear from our callers."

When the first caller starts with, "What is up with Adams? Is his new girl distracting him?" I stab the off button.

"It's not her fault," I mutter to the unknown caller. "It's mine."

And I hope my teammates aren't as disappointed in me as I am. But they have every right to be.

When I walk through the corridor of the practice facility, my heart feels heavy. My feet do too. I dread heading into the locker room.

I let these guys down yesterday, so when I tug open the door, I brace myself for their disappointment.

"Hey, Adams," Rand calls out, patting his stubbly cheek. "Check it out. No shave."

Clements tips his chin my way and lobs a yellow hacky sack at me.

I catch it easily. "New one?"

"Fuck yes. We're gonna start a new streak. Isn't that right?"

Rand nods enthusiastically. "Starting now."

The running back points at me. "My game was off yesterday, bro. I should have caught a couple of those throws. But today? Today, I woke up early and did yoga. Nama-fucking-ste. I've got peace about the game yesterday, and now we're gonna concentrate on fucking up Dallas this weekend on our turf."

Holy shit. What did I do to deserve a team like this? Their attitudes are everything. I fight off a grin so I don't look too happy about losing, but I'm ecstatic that they aren't blaming me. It was a tough loss all around.

But I still want them to know how seriously I take my job. I clear my throat. "Thanks, guys. I've been beating myself up. I know I played badly yesterday, and I'm sorry I let you down, but I'm ready to put it behind us and kick ass."

Clements scoffs. "Dude, it was one bad game. We were all off."

"We all have them," Rand echoes. "It's a new day."

It is, and I've got a new attitude—all football, all the time.

When we head to the video room to watch clips from yesterday, Coach pats me on the shoulder. "Let's find our focus again, men," he says.

Then, he breaks down each key play, pointing out what went wrong.

Not enough coverage.

Snap took too long.

No one was open.

Missed a tackle.

The Hawks' defense is tight.

Their QB was on fire.

Coach isn't cold, just clinical. With each assessment, I shed a little bit more weight off my shoulders. I didn't play great, but the other team sure did. It wasn't my best game, but it wasn't any of our best games.

When he hits end on the video, he points to the

field. "Time for drills. We've got a game to win on Sunday."

I smack palms with my guys then trot out to practice, ready to leave the Hawks game behind me.

I need to put everything behind me, and out of my head.

Even this empty ache in my heart.

An ache that intensifies when I go home that night alone.

Instantly, I miss her all over again. I wish I were seeing her tonight. Making dinner with her. Talking in her kitchen. Curling up with her in her bed.

But I don't reach out. I hit the hay early.

* * *

On Tuesday morning, I peel off my best time running in a while, but I feel out of sorts all day. Even after an excellent practice. Even though the team looks damn good.

That night I go home alone again—of course—but my condo feels emptier than it ever has before. I text Carter and shoot the breeze with him for a while, then we play a few rounds of basketball on my Xbox.

When we're done, I check my phone, wishing for a note from Brooke.

But she offered to cool things for me, for my

fucking benefit so I could do the job I'm paid to do. And I took her up on a generous, selfless offer.

She's not going to reach out since she did this *for* me.

She's a woman of her word.

I should be a man who gets his job done.

I go to bed alone, the same damn way I wake up the next day. I do it all over again. Lather, rinse, repeat.

Practice, focus, miss Brooke.

Then miss her again, and again, and again.

After practice Thursday morning, I head out to meet my agent for lunch, trying to shake off the hollow feeling chasing me—my guilt too. It's the day of the press tour. I should be there to show the bloggers and podcasters around. They've been good to me. I should be good back to them.

Maddox waits for me at the Indian food truck. When he heard I didn't get to try it a few weeks ago, he insisted on taking me out.

I stride up to Maddox and say hello, focusing on the here and now. I will be present for lunch with my agent. "I am here to repent," I say, flashing him a smile.

"Good. The chana masala will make you never

ditch this truck again," he says, then asks if he can order for me.

"Hell, yes. You always know what to pick," I say.

He orders naan, eggplant bharta and the aforementioned chana masala, then we grab a picnic table.

As we tuck into the tasty dishes, he asks about my mom. "She's keeping busy with Sophie and Mira, I presume?"

"She is." This is one of the things I've always loved about Maddox. He cares about me beyond my performance on the field.

As we eat, we chat about my family, then he says, "And what are you thinking you want to do when your contract is up at the end of the season? Renew?"

My stomach dips with new nerves. "If they'll have me."

He furrows his brow, clearly surprised I said that. "Pretty sure they'll have you. I can't make any promises, but you're one of the top quarterbacks in the league." He tilts his head, studies me. "What's going on, Drew?"

I'm so used to being the confident guy with him, showing him I belong in the sport, that I'm worthy of the contracts he inks. Usually that's all I need to be. But my emotions are seeping through the cracks today. I'm still unsure if I made the right choice on Monday morning.

But I don't need to burden Maddox with that.

"Nothing really," I say, but I can hear the lie in my voice.

Maddox must too, since he sets down his fork with purpose. "What's really going on, and how can I help you?"

I don't want to be the guy who complains about his lady woes. But I can't keep it from him, especially since he seems to be figuring it out already.

"Just woman trouble," I say, trying to make light of it.

He looks concerned. "Did something go wrong with Brooke?"

He knows I was seeing her, since our pics were all over socials.

I heave a sigh, then let a little more of the truth out. "Yeah. And it's probably all my fault." Fuck, that's a relief to say.

But I just miss her ridiculously.

"What are you going to do about it?"

That is the question, but I've got zero answers. "I don't know, Maddox. I thought maybe I was distracted because of her. And I was supposed to do this press tour with the team today. She got me out of it. But it's not in my nature to back out."

"It's not. That's not your style. You work hard and you represent," he says. "But is that what's eating at you?"

I scratch my jaw, then shake my head. "Yes, but mostly I just miss her."

He gives a soft smile. "And have you talked to Carter about that?"

I give him a quizzical look. "Why do you ask?"

"He's always the one you talk to about your romantic woes. He usually knows what you should do."

Maybe I've avoided talking to him about Brooke these last few days. For that very reason.

But I can change that right away.

25

THURSDAY AFTERNOON QUARTERBACK

Brooke

Drew and I never went parasailing, but even so, I shift my gaze away from the parasailer floating above the ocean. It reminds me of the day we met.

I don't need any reminders of the conversations we had, the way we flirted, or our instant connection.

I'm at an oceanfront café Thursday afternoon with Cara. I worked from home this morning, and I'll be heading to the stadium for the tour shortly. But first, lunch. We're celebrating that Cara just aced one of her key exams.

"I'll say it again—I'm seriously proud of you." I toast with the remains of my iced tea one last time as we wrap up.

"And I'm amazed by you," she says.

I arch a brow in question. "What do you mean?"

"We've eaten a full meal and you haven't mentioned Drew once. You have some serious restraint."

I sigh heavily. "There's no point. There's nothing to say."

Except my heart aches still, and that sucks. The only thing that's taken my mind away from him is work. I've logged twelve hours most days. All the work reminds me that I'm closer to paying off my loans.

And it's better to worry about loans than a real fake romance. Or a fake real romance? Or whatever it was.

I raise my chin, take a hearty sip of the last of my iced tea, and set down the glass. "And on that note, I have to give a tour to the press."

"Why are you doing the tour? You're a lawyer," she says.

It's a damn good question. Originally, Stephen just wanted me to be part of the event because I handled all the deals with the food vendors. But then he wanted me on it because of Drew. Now, I'm leading the dang thing. "Nancy in publicity is out sick for the day, so Stephen asked me to fill in. Plus, he says I'm the best at only saying to the press exactly what he wants said. Yay me."

"Well, you're pretty damn sharp, Miss Legal Eagle. Maybe you should have Nancy's job," she says.

I shudder. "No thanks. Contracts are my speed. But it's just one tour, so it'll be fine."

I stand to go but Cara grabs my arm, gently pulling me back into my chair. "What if they ask about the two of you?"

My throat tightens. "I'll say something...pithy about how football requires focus."

Though that sounds horribly canned. Also, it's a lie. Plenty of athletes can handle romance and work. Plenty of humans can. I'd thought we could.

But I was wrong.

"Brooke, his bad game isn't your fault," Cara says.

"What do you mean?" I ask.

"You actually believe it's your fault. You buy into this whole focus blah-blah-blah. But it's bullshit."

Whoa. Cara hardly ever swears. "Tell me what you really think."

"You saw the game on Sunday, right?" she asks, a blazing intensity in her eyes.

"Of course."

"And did San Francisco not play its ass off in that game?"

We are both football daughters. Cara knows the game inside and out like I do. "They were great," I agree.

"No one was going to beat them. He's an idiot if he thinks he lost because of you. The Hawks were relentless. They played a tight, intense game, and they took advantage of every opportunity."

Can't argue there. "But it's not my place to convince him of that."

"I know. But I don't want you thinking you rattled him. He had a bad game. It happens. Don't put it on you, and don't let him put it on you."

Cara makes a good argument. One I should share —not to win Drew back, but because it's true and because it matters.

Sometimes you win; sometimes you lose. A pro baller knows how to play through life's ups and downs, the bad times and the good times.

Drew's not just any pro baller.

He's a damn good one. He needs to have faith in himself. Maybe he needs to know others have faith in him too, even if he has one imperfect game.

When I see him again, I'll tell him as much. Only, I have no idea when that'll be.

After I go home, change, and head to the stadium, I decide I'm not going to leave this moment to chance.

26

THE REAL STREAK

Drew

Carter can't stop laughing. He goes on for thirty seconds and once he's done gasping for breath, he points at me over FaceTime in case I didn't realize I was the butt of a joke. "I wish I'd recorded that. I'd play it at your wedding."

I jerk my head back, staring hard at his face on the screen. "What are you talking about?"

"That whole thing you just said. *I walked away from the best relationship I've ever had because I can't handle being an adult.*"

I groan. "That is not what I said."

"But that's what I heard," he says, laughing once again.

I stop pacing around my condo and drop my

head into my hand. "Why did Maddox tell me to talk to you? Is he a prankster?"

Carter scoffs. "Because he knew I'd tell you the cold, hard truth," he says, turning starkly serious. "You didn't fuck up a game because you fell in love. It was just a game, man. One that you didn't happen to win. Don't throw the woman out with the L."

I blink and shake my head like a dog shaking off water. "What did you just say?"

He repeats the part about the game, but I gesture for him to back it up. "The other part."

"Oh," he says with a laugh. "The part about you being in love? Yeah, that's why you're all weird and shit. You're in love with her, and you freaked out. And you totally can fucking handle football and love. You're a pro baller, so go out and do it."

I take a moment to let the weight of his words sink in. Then I check the time.

Oh, fuck.

Then, as I spin into action, I spot a silver charm on my nightstand, and it gives me an idea.

Traffic sucks.

"C'mon," I mutter as I check the clock on the dashboard for the fiftieth time. I've got ten more minutes to go one mile.

It could take an hour, or it could take a few minutes.

Most likely it will feel like a year.

But luck shines down on me, and I cover the final mile in eight minutes, pulling into the players' lot and snagging the first spot I see.

I grab my phone without checking my messages, without calling Brooke. I don't want to do this on the phone. I want to see her in person.

And I want to be a man of my word.

I said I'd do the tour, and when you say you're going to do something, you should damn well do it.

I run to the players' entrance then downstairs to the corridor that leads to the locker room, where the tour starts. I pick up the pace until I spot a group milling around the door one hundred feet ahead—twenty or so reporters, then Clements, then...

There she is.

Wow.

She looks stunning, and I'm such an idiot for letting her go.

I don't slow down.

I've got ten seconds to be on time, and I'm going to fucking be on time for my commitments.

Especially the one I made to Brooke when I told her I was falling for her. Part and parcel of that is I won't want to cool off again.

She spots me, looking at me as if I'm as unex-pected as a housecat wandering through the stadium. Her head tilts, her brow furrows, and her face is unreadable. Her poker face is tight, but her brown eyes are full of questions and, I think, hope.

I can't take my eyes off her. She's gorgeous in her black skirt and red blouse, her blonde hair twisted up on her head.

But it's her heart that I want most—the heart that wanted to give me space.

Fuck space.

I don't want that anymore.

I'm about to run past all these reporters when a guy in glasses speaks first, stopping me. "Hey, Drew. We didn't think you were going to be here."

A redheaded woman with freckles goes next. "Are you joining the tour after all, Drew?"

Then Clements strides forward and gives me a fist bump. "Always showing me up," he says with a smirk.

"Thanks for being my backup," I say, but I'm not in the mood to joke.

I've got eyes for one person and one person only.

"I'd love to show you all around," I say to the reporters, my gaze locked on Brooke's. "But there's something I have to do first."

I walk past them all, and they part, letting me reach her quickly.

She purses her lips and waits for me.

I reach into my pocket, take out the charm neck-lace, and press it into her hand. "I love you. I want you to leave this at my place any time, and I'll keep finding it and bringing it to you."

Instantly, her bluff vanishes. She smiles like a Jumbotron caught us kissing.

Which sounds like a damn good idea but I'm not done. "I want football *and* romance. I was a fool to think we couldn't make both work. I don't want any space from you. I want to see you every night, and every morning."

But before she can speak, I realize my faux pas. "Oh, shit," I whisper. "You probably didn't want me to say all that in public."

With her free hand, she grabs the collar of my shirt. "I do. I did. All I want is you."

I loop my arms around her neck. "I'm sorry," I whisper. "But thank you for giving me another chance."

"Drew," she says, her voice soft and feathery and just for me. "You'll have bad days at work, and so will I. But we'll have good days too. We just can't let the bad days dictate how we feel about each other."

I nod, still a little guilty, but that's okay. I should feel guilty. I fucked up when I freaked out. But I can learn from it. "I know. I believe that. I didn't think there was room for love and football, but I was wrong."

"I want love and football too," she says.

"Oh my God, just fucking kiss her," Clements breaks in with an aggrieved groan.

The guy with glasses chimes, "Yes, yes, yes!"

The woman cheers me on too. "Right now."

I look at Brooke, asking permission. "Are you sure?"

She laughs. "Trust me, it's no hardship to kiss you in public *or* private. But first, maybe put this on me?"

She hands me the charm necklace, and I loop it around her neck, clasping it. Out of the corner of my eye, I see the phone cameras go wild. Pretty sure they've been going wild this whole time.

Works for me.

This moment is as real as all the other ones—the Whac-A-Mole game, the walk after the charity event, the kiss on the beach.

But this one is the start of the real us.

My heart beats faster as I move in closer. Then my lips are on hers, and I kiss the woman I love.

But not for long. We have a tour to do.

When I break the kiss, she's smiling like she has a secret.

"What's that for?" I ask.

"Oh, I just love you too," she says. Then she clears her throat, and meets the eyes of the press, who've caught all this on camera. "Let me show you the locker room first."

Just like that, we give a tour of the stadium together.

* * *

When it's over, she grabs my hand, pulls me into a stairwell, and kisses me hard. "I can't believe you showed up here like that."

"I can't believe I didn't show up three days ago. I'm so sorry," I say, wishing I could have gotten my act together. "And I'll keep saying that. You deserve to hear it. You deserve everything good in the world, Brooke."

Shaking her head, she presses her finger to my lips. "We're good. No groveling is necessary. I get it."

My heart thumps harder. She's too good to me. "You really do?"

"Drew, you had a great start to the season. You had all sorts of luck, but it came from talent and hard work. Then you had one rough game. But you blamed yourself when the reality is...it's just football."

That's what I started realizing the other day in the locker room with my guys. But hearing her say that means a lot to me too. That's another form of luck—when the person you love completely understands you.

"Took me a while to figure that out," I say.

"You were doing a lot. You've taken on a ton of extra responsibilities. It can be overwhelming. Just know I'm here for you. And I know you'll do great this weekend," she says, then studies my face. Her eyes are full of question marks. "Didn't you get my message?"

She sent me one? Of course she fucking did because she's awesome. "I didn't look at my phone. I was in such a rush to get here and see you." I grab it from my pocket and click on it, reading words she sent a little while ago.

Streaks never last. It's the very nature of streaks to end. But I believe in you as an athlete and as a man. You've handled this season so far with grace and confidence, and I know you'll keep doing it.

My heart thunders. "I don't deserve you. But I want to deserve you." Then I kiss her again, reveling in the sweet taste of her lips, the scent of her hair, the feel of her in my arms once more.

She kisses me back tenderly, as if she's delighting in this kiss too. Like she's savoring every second of us coming back together.

But I'm also getting turned on, so I end it. "I should go, or I might try to hike up your skirt here in the stairwell."

She wiggles a brow. Such a naughty woman. "I probably wouldn't stop you."

I groan, wanting that badly. "All the more reason for me to take off. So I can get you off later. When do you finish work?"

"In a couple of hours."

It feels like an eternity. "Can I bury my face between your legs then?"

She smiles. "Only if you have a soundtrack for me."

* * *

That evening, I'm in my favorite place. On Brooke's bed, my hands sliding along her soft thighs as I devour her, making her lose her mind to pleasure.

She arches and writhes against me, swearing like a dirty woman who loves sex.

I am having the time of my life.

I grip her ass as I go down on her, determined to take her over the edge.

Seconds later, she's gripping my skull and coming undone with a loud cry.

I slow my pace, kiss her once more, than wipe a hand across my mouth. When she blinks open her eyes, she looks dazed and blissed out. She takes out her ear buds. Smiles. Sighs. Flops her head back on the pillow. "Wow."

"Wow to you," I say, then press a kiss to her belly.

She laughs again, then pushes up on her elbows, wicked deeds in her eyes.

"My turn," she says, so eager and hungry.

She is my woman. My perfect match.

"I like the sound of that." But first I bring her close, kiss her cheek, then say, "You're the streak I don't want to break."

EPILOGUE

ANY TIPS FOR ME?

Drew

Brooke comes to my game that weekend.

That's not surprising. She's been to all my home games. But this time, she sits on the fifty-yard line with Patrick and Cara. When I run out to the field, I wave to her.

She waves back then points to her jersey. Number Eight.

I love it, I mouth, then add, *I love you*.

Then, I play ball. In between possessions, Gabe and I kick the hacky sack, keeping up his ritual.

And by the end of the game, we've returned to *our* ritual—winning.

As victory flashes on the scoreboard, I high-five

the guys. Last weekend is behind me. I don't have to be perfect all the time. I just have to try my best.

These guys know I do that. I play hard for them, for the fans, and for the whole city.

But also for the woman I love.

After I chat with a sideline reporter, I run over to Brooke, kiss her, then pull her into my arms on the field.

"I told you so," I say with a smile.

Rolling her eyes, she laughs. "Yes, Drew. You sure did."

I pepper her with more kisses, so damn glad she's here and that I can kiss her freely at last in front of anyone and everyone.

But there's someone I want her to meet.

* * *

My family heads into the café first, and I let the door close behind them. I reach for Brooke's hand, squeeze it. "I'm pretty excited for you to meet my mom," I say.

"News flash—me too."

We walk in together. When I find my mom at a table, I smile and Mom waves back, then stands up.

"Mom, I want to introduce you to my girlfriend," I say.

"The one you were wrong about when you didn't

think you could have love and football?" she asks innocently.

That sounds awfully familiar.

"Mom! Are you reading the gossip about us?" I ask. That's exactly what I said to Brooke before the stadium tour.

She rolls her eyes. "Sweetheart, everyone knows." She extends a hand to Brooke. "Thank you for putting up with him."

My girlfriend laughs. "It's truly my pleasure."

When Mom looks away to check on my sisters, Brooke winks at me and whispers, "It is *my* pleasure."

Then, before we sit, I tug her back and whisper, "I'm spanking you later for that."

"I should hope so," she says.

Over dinner, I ask my mom if she has any game tips for me.

"Yes." Mom looks to Brooke, smiles sagely. "Don't let her go."

I don't plan to.

ANOTHER EPILOGUE

ALL OF THE ABOVE

Brooke

Springtime

The sun warms my shoulders as I turn the pages in my new book.

It's a perfect day to bask on the beach and enjoy the ocean breeze. When I finish a chapter in the new Rhys Locke spy novel, I set down the book and gaze out at the water as boarders ride the waves.

"Your paddle boarding days are well and truly over," I say to Drew, a little sad for him.

But it's hard to stay sad when life is so good.

Including days like this. He's by my side, reading too, and he sets down his book. "Oh, well. At least I was able to hit the waves when it mattered."

I rub the back of his head with affection,

picturing that fateful and wonderful day before the season started. "Back when I could save you."

He leans in closer, nuzzling my neck. "A dude in distress needs his damsel. Or really, his lifeguard surf angel nurse rock star goddess," he says.

There will be no more saving because paddle boarding is off-limits for Drew for a long time now.

As in, the next five years. After he finished the season with a 13–5 record and took the team to the championship series, the Mercenaries signed him to a five-year contract with a no-trade clause. His agent is quite a dealmaker, and Drew took Maddox and me out for a fantastic dinner in Venice Beach a few months ago to celebrate. Then, Maddox told us that he's leaving to join a new agency and he wants to take Drew with him.

Drew's answer was pure Drew—*you're not getting rid of me, buddy*.

"Good. I don't want to get rid of you," he'd said.

I'm not surprised. Maddox takes good care of my guy, and I appreciate all he does. He's become a friend too, and we often share reading recs and hit the bookstore in Venice together, since he lives here too. I can't wait to hear what happens when he starts his new gig, and if it opens new doors for him.

Maybe even to love.

Or perhaps I just have romance on my mind.

And happy endings, since the Mercenaries love Drew, just like the fans do.

But not as much as I do.

He might belong to the team, and he might belong to the city, but in the morning, and then later at the end of the night, Drew belongs to me. You might even say we have *two-a-days*. He moved in with me a few months ago, and when he comes home from practice, we cook together. Or we talk. Or we fuck.

Sometimes, we do all of the above.

Who am I kidding? Most nights, we do all of the above.

Tonight, though, we're going to the pier to play some games. It's kind of our thing—Skee-Ball and Whac-A-Mole and movies. And talking endlessly about all of them.

We pack up as the sun fades, then after I shower and change, we head to Santa Monica.

Out on the pier, as the moon rises in the spring sky, I take him on in a game of Whac-A-Mole. "I will reign victorious," I shout.

I raise the mallet to pound one of the critters, but I don't see Drew.

Where did he go?

When I spin around, mallet in hand, I gasp.

He's on one knee, a velvet box in his hand, his hazel eyes flickering with vulnerability and hope.

Is this real?

My heart thunders. My bones sing.

Yes, this is so damn real I'm trembling with happiness already.

"Brooke Holland, I love playing games with you every day and every night," he says, his tone solemn and full of tenderness too. I'll remember the way he sounds right now always. "You challenge me, you make me a better man, and you make me so damn happy."

"You make me so happy too," I say, my voice breaking with joy.

"Will you be my wife?"

My heart climbs up my throat as I nod over and over, and I just can't stop. "Yes, yes, yes. I would love to marry you."

When he flicks open the box, a brilliant diamond shines brightly at me as the moon glows on the stone. "It's perfect for you," he says reverently.

I sink to the ground as he slides it on my finger. "You're perfect for me," I say, emotions overflowing.

He cups my cheeks, kisses my lips, then smiles— that blinding smile that caught my eye the day I met him. That holds my attention every morning and every night.

Then he says, "I guess some guys do have all the luck."

Patrick

That   Night   At   the   Movie   Theater   Several Months Ago

You think you've got it together. That you can give your buddy hell about anything and everything. That you're too cool to be affected by things like crushes, and then whammo.

You see a woman who takes your breath away.

When I walk into the movie theater, I try not to gawk at the gorgeous blonde at the popcorn counter.

I'm sure I'm failing.

I have to be failing.

But fuck it.

I'll fail.

Her jeans celebrate her legs like they were made to praise her figure. Her V-neck blouse dips dangerously low over the curve of her breasts but not low enough all at the same time. Her rosebud lips are divinely kissable, and maybe I'm having a religious experience because I want to worship at the altar of her body all night long and into the next day too.

Then her eyes meet mine and fuck it. I'm a goner.

Consider me officially in a state of crush.

Finally, I turn my attention back to my friend, but it seems he's also been converted to the Church of Babeism. Drew's gaze has snagged on the woman in the pink dress—the one who posed by the banner with him at the meet and greet. She smiles at him.

"Hey, Adams," Brooke says to my buddy. "Good to see you."

"And you too," he says. But I'm staring stupidly at the other woman. Fortunately, I *should* be looking at her since Brooke is introducing her. "This is my sister, Cara."

And the pretty blonde with the button nose shoots me a *you're busted* look. "And you two must be the guys planning clown pranks," she says.

I desperately try to think of something witty to say, but I'm pretty sure I was giving Drew hell about a movie. Oh, and plotting clown pranks. Well, he was planning to send one to get me, and now this woman is going to know I am fucking afraid of clowns. *Real cool, Patrick.*

But I go with it. I use...yup...clowns as an opening line. I adopt a serious look. "For the record, I am vehemently opposed to clown pranks. And to clowns."

She hums in understanding. "I get that. Completely."

"Well, clearly this was meant to be," I say, hoping to make the best of our clown fear. "I believe we just clown bonded."

She laughs. "Yes. It's totally a thing. Tell me more about your least-favorite clowns."

"The ones with red hair. Big noses and huge feet," I say, moving next to her at the counter.

She clasps her chest. "Those are my least favorite too."

Cara laughs, then says to Drew and me, "Are you two clowns heading to see *Fake Play*?"

Oh, hell yes. *Thank you, fate.* "We are." We've already clown bonded. Time to seize this chance. "Would you like to sit together? In case there are clowns or anything in the flick, we can support each other through it."

Cara sets a hand on her chest. "I was really worried about clowns in the movie, so that'd be great."

She turns to Brooke, asking if she's okay with it, and when she says yes, I buy two popcorns.

As Brooke and Drew catch up, I ask Cara if she's seen *Fake Play* before.

"It's my sister's favorite, so she's forced me to watch it a few times."

"It's not your thing?"

"I like it..." she says, hedging.

"But?"

She looks guilty. "I'm a secret documentary geek."

Shut the front door. This is too much. Too perfect. "Me too."

She scoffs. "No way."

"You doubt me now?"

"I mean, what are the chances we both like documentaries, and dislike clowns?"

"True, true. Those are just signs of good taste. We

won't know unless we put this documentary like to the test. I might like military documentaries and you might like nature ones, and where would we be then?"

She gasps. "You're right. It's the documentary quandary." She shoots me a flirty look. "I'll tell you mine if you tell me yours."

All sorts of dirty things I want her to tell me flit through my head, but they're far too X-rated for a documentary conversation. "Animals," I reply instead, naming one of my favorite kinds of documentaries.

She laughs with sheer delight, it seems. "Who doesn't like animal documentaries?"

"People with no soul." I shudder.

"And, for the record, my favorite kind of documentary—aside from the animal features—are the really twisty news-style ones."

And this seems like the best beginning in the history of meeting women ever because, "Me too," I say. "Have you seen *F Boys And Girls*?" I ask, referencing a recent Webflix special about a group of reality show stars who conned a long line of networks to get on their shows.

"Yes!" she says, her eyes widening. "It was guilty but addictive viewing."

I lean closer, catch a drift of her honeysuckle scent. "I couldn't agree more," I say, only my voice comes out a little rough, a little gravelly, and I don't even care if Drew hears and gives me shit about it later because I'm having too much goddamn fun.

"No clowns and the very specific twisty news documentaries," Cara says, tilting her head toward me as we head toward our seats. "Sounds like we're a match made in movie heaven."

And she doesn't need to tell me twice.

The four of us sit, with Cara next to me, chatting about some of our other favorite documentaries as the trailers roll on the screen. Then the lights dim, and the movie begins.

I was giving Drew a hard time about the flick. Yes, he's the hardcore movie fan, but truly it's not bad, especially when the hero realizes he's been into the heroine all along.

I just met Cara, so it doesn't feel like a mirror into my life, but what does match my emotions is the hero's decision to go for it.

That's how I feel.

Normally I don't dive into romance or dates. I'm cautious. I research, like I do with investments.

But sometimes you just feel chemistry. Sometimes you have so much in common with someone that it's worth taking a chance on them, even if it means risking heartbreak on the other side.

So after the movie ends and we're all on Ocean Avenue, I say, "Want to grab a beer? Shave ice? Smoothie?"

The question is for everyone, since I don't want to

be rude, but truly, I hope Cara's game.

She smiles brightly, eyes twinkling like she's just as excited as I am to keep up this unexpectedly fantastic impromptu date. "Definitely."

But Brooke yawns, and my chest tightens.

"It's past your bedtime," Cara jumps in, teasing. "It's already nine."

"Yes, someone has been working early and late," Brooke says, with another yawn. "But I don't mind if you want to stay."

"I'll drive you home," Cara says, and my heart takes a little *don't go* nosedive even though I like that she's taking care of her sister.

"I'll drive you, Brooke," my buddy steps in to save the day, and I should never have played with his text messages that time because the man is clearly a saint.

As Cara and Brooke say goodbye, Drew claps me on the back. "Have fun, buddy. And don't forget to tell her I win the prank wars."

"Yeah, that'll be our topic of conversation for sure," I reply, because I just can't help needling him one last time.

As Brooke and Drew walk toward his car, I gesture toward the smoothie store on the corner, its bright lights spilling out onto the sidewalk. "Smoothies are calling our names."

"Is it the berries calling to you? Do you prefer banana? Pineapple?" she asks as we walk.

"All of the above," I reply. "I'm smoothie-omnivorous."

She clasps a hand dramatically to her chest. "I'm a mango or bust gal." She faux shudders. "And here I thought we had everything in common."

"Ah, but it's good to be different in some ways," I reply, laughing at her antics. "Like work, for example. I can't imagine you're a financial advisor too?"

"No," she replies as we stop in front of the store. "I'm studying to be a special ed teacher."

"Wow," I reply, impressed. "What made you choose that?"

She shrugs, her eyes turning serious for a beat. "I had great teachers myself and I always wanted to teach. It was as simple as that."

"You're pretty amazing. You know that, right?" I ask, a little gentle, a lot intrigued.

She looks up at me. Tension crackles in the air between us. My eyes are drawn to her lips, those rosebuds tempting me, taunting me. She darts her tongue out, leaves them glistening, and I ache to do the same.

But she suddenly looks down, turns back to the store. "Want to order?" she asks, and the moment evaporates as we head to the counter and order our drinks.

A few minutes later, we're back on the street, the beach to our left, the city to our right. The scent of the ocean fills my lungs as she asks me about my job, and I tell her about the investments I make and how I research, research, research to ensure I'm prepared for whatever scenario may arise in the rapidly fluctuating market.

"That's another thing we have in common. This right here?" Cara taps her purse as we walk past a group of people singing Drew's team's song. "I've got Band-Aids. Tissues. Ibuprofen. I like to be prepared too."

I grin and gesture to the sandy shores beside us. "And what about the beach? Do you happen to like moonlit walks along the beach as well?"

"What a coincidence. I do." She laughs and her hand glances over my arm, and goddamn, one simple touch shouldn't affect me so much, but it does.

We walk past couples holding hands, couples with their arms around each other, couples, couples, couples, and it seems only too natural to say, "Do you know what else I like, Cara?"

She stops walking, glances up at me from under her impossibly long lashes. "Tell me."

"You," I say simply.

Pink colors her cheeks, but she doesn't look away. "Looks like that's another thing we have in common then," she replies on a whisper, and fuck it. I know I should spend more time getting to know her, doing my research, but maybe that's where I've gone wrong in the past. Maybe this—

acting on a newfound crush—is the way that's right.

She licks her lower lip, and I don't miss the moment this time. I cup her jaw, my hand gliding over her soft skin, and lean in to place a gentle kiss on her lips. Her hands wrap around my waist as she sort of sighs into my mouth, like this moment is just too perfect, too much.

I linger, not wanting the kiss to end. She tastes like mangos and the magic of this whirlwind movie-turned-date, and she parts her lips, inviting me in for more, more, more, and I greedily accept.

When we finally pull apart, her chest rises and falls against mine, and my cock is more than ready to take things back to her place, my place, *any* goddamn place where we can be alone. Turns out instant crushes are my new favorite thing. Nothing could kill this buzz.

"I have to go," Cara says, and places one hand on my chest. "Home. Alone."

Well, okay then.

Maybe that could kill the buzz a little.

"Of course," I reply, because I'm not an asshole. If the lady wants to leave, she can leave. But... "I'd like to see you again. Why don't you come over for a documentary-and-dinner date tomorrow night?"

Her eyes blink to the waves crashing down on the beach, then flick back to meet mine, an ocean of uncertainty in her gaze. "I'm sorry, Patrick. This is happening really fast for me. I had a bad experience with an ex and I just..."

My heart plummets to the bottom of the board-walk. I step back. "I get it. Don't worry."

"No." She shakes her head, grabs my hand. "I do want this. But we'd need to take things slowly. I've only known you a few hours and already I feel like this could be something between us—but I don't want to risk getting hurt again."

Phew. So she does want more—and more with me.

And for moments like we've shared tonight, I'm willing to do whatever it takes.

I tuck a strand of her blonde hair behind her ear, my hand lingering there. "We can go slow. Turtle slow."

She smiles up at me, but it's not as brilliant as it was before, as if the memory of her ex has somehow dulled the spark between us. "Thank you."

"No. Thank you," I say, "for taking a chance on me."

And as we exchange numbers, I know two things for certain.

One: I'm all about instant crushes now. This is the best night I've had in a very long time.

And two: even though she's agreed to a date, this somehow feels like a breakup.

Cara

There's a fine line between too much and just enough.

Take frosting, for example. Too much and it overwhelms the cake, smooshing all over your face as you try to eat. The balance is wrong. It's no longer fun.

That's how I view dating. Too much and it can feel less like a recipe for romance, more like an overfrosted cupcake.

It's difficult, messy, and not fun at all.

"But you really like the guy," Taylor says as I sit at the bar, where I've arrived five minutes early for my next date with Patrick. She places a napkin with a glass of water on it in front of me, ever the polished bar professional. "Did you want to order a drink now or wait till he's here?"

"I'll wait, thanks," I reply. "And I know. I do like him. We had this chemistry that was pure magic. And that kiss..." I sigh into my water and take a long sip. That kiss was one week ago, but it's been replaying in my mind under the heading of Most Romantic Kiss Ever since.

"So what's the problem then?" she asks, grabbing a glass from the dishwasher and polishing it.

"I just..." I shrug. "I guess I'm scared. When I started college, I dated this guy I met on campus. And he seemed perfect on paper—like we had everything in common." I shudder at the memory. "Turns out that was because he'd researched my likes and dislikes. He turned himself into this mirror of me, and when I started to pull away, he wouldn't leave me alone."

"Oh, Cara." Tay places a hand over mine. She's a newer friend in my circle, but has rapidly proved to be a good one. "That must have been scary."

"It was. He'd show up unannounced, text me all the time—he even followed me places a few times and tried to laugh it off, like it was just a big coincidence." I shudder at the memory. "That's all in the past now, but I guess it's made it harder for me to take someone like Patrick at face value."

"That makes sense, sweetie." Taylor places the glass on the shelf and grabs another, running the cloth over it with practiced efficiency. "But not every man will be like your ex."

"I know," I reply, sitting up a little straighter. "Which is why I'm doing this. We're taking things slow, and I'm taking a chance."

And when Patrick walks into the bar, I'm so very glad I am.

At the movies, he wore jeans, but this evening he's come straight from work. I didn't know I was the kind of woman who cared what a man wore, but now that I've seen him in this tailored navy-blue suit, I'm rapidly becoming all about the three-piece, *thankyouverymuch*.

His dark eyes search the room, and when they land on me I feel it—that *zing* that thrilled through me when we laughed and joked on the beach.

He walks closer, a charming smile on his face, and when he kisses me on the cheek, it sends tingles to my toes.

"It's good to see you again," he says, pulling back and standing close to me, one arm resting on the bar.

Chemistry sizzles in the air between us. I place my hand over his. "It really is," I say, and I've never meant those words so much.

Conversation flows between us and soon, one drink turns into two turns into coffee and cake—but I call it a night before I get too swept up in this man who seems to be okay with taking it slow for me.

One week later, we go mini golfing at a cute retro course. When I score my first ever hole in one, he lifts me up in the air, twirls me around, and whoops like he's never seen anyone whack a golf ball before.

On our next date, we go to a terrarium lab. As we layer rocks and ferns into little glass jars, creating our very own mini greenhouses, it feels a little like we're building something else. Something bigger.

And more than a month after we first met, I can't hold back any longer. He's taken it slow for me. He's given me the space and time I needed—but I can't keep worrying forever. He's not too good to be true—he is true.

And it seems like he's mine.

I just have to take a chance on love.

Patrick

One year later

"You've been a very naughty boy, Patrick."

I pause in adjusting my tie in the en suite mirror and smile. That voice coming from the bedroom can only mean one of two things.

Either Cara has found the gift I left out for her or she's about to make all my dirty student/teacher fantasies come true.

I stroll into the bedroom, and I shouldn't stare, shouldn't still be affected by her like this, but fuck it.

I just am.

She stands by the bed in simple black lace lingerie, her gorgeous body bared for me to see. It doesn't matter how many times I explore it with my hands, my lips, my tongue...I always want more.

Like now.

Like right motherfucking now.

I step closer and slide my hands around her waist, her smooth skin so soft, then I lean down and kiss that rosebud mouth. She sighs into the kiss, melts into my body, and I pull her closer, closer still until there's no space between us, no gap that separates me from her—there's just *us*.

Her tongue darts into my mouth. I meet it stroke for stroke, turning this kiss from a simple *oh hi there* into a hot and heady dream. We kiss like two people hungry for more, hungry for each other.

The softness of her hair is like a dream as I curl it around my hand, tug it slightly, and then—

Oh, shit.

I stop, pull away.

"What's wrong?" Cara asks, two adorable little lines furrowing between her brows.

"Did I ruin your wedding hair?" I ask, checking over her shoulder to see if I've undone all the hairstylist's good work. "Nope. Still looks amazing. Close one." I wipe a bead of imaginary sweat from my brow, but I take a step back.

It's one thing to play a prank on your best bud every now and then.

It's another entirely to fuck with his wedding day, and I won't delay Brooke's walk down the aisle because I've ruined her maid of honor's hairstyle.

"Thank you for protecting me," Cara says, grinning as she takes the silky blue dress from the bed and slips it on. It effortlessly curves around her body, cinching in at the waist and draping in all the right places, and I let loose a low whistle.

"Wow," I mutter. "You're such a knockout."

"Wait till you see me in a wedding dress," Cara teases, flashing me the diamond that sparkles on her ring finger, and I grin.

"About that..." I gesture to the gift-wrapped box on the bedside table. "I believe you were about to reprimand me for misbehaving?"

She grins. "I was. You didn't have to get me a gift."

"That's the beauty of gifts." I shrug. "They're not a *have to*. They're a *want to*."

She lifts the lid on the blue box and lets loose a small gasp. "Patrick," she breathes, then lifts the necklace so it dangles in the light. It's a slight silver chain with a small charm on it—the symbol for infinity.

"I know it's a little corny, but..." I shrug, take the necklace from her hands, and do the clasp up at her nape. "You're my forever, Cara. And I wanted to remind you of that."

"Thank you," she says, spinning in my arms to kiss me once again, this time a little softer, a little more chaste, but no less loaded with meaning. "I can't wait to marry you and be your wife."

"Thirty days can't come fast enough," I agree, holding her close.

And as we finish getting ready to watch two of the most important people in our lives getting married, I've never felt happier.

I might be afraid of clowns.

I might be hesitant to take major risks.

But there's one thing I'm one hundred percent confident in, and it's the woman holding hands with me in our hotel suite.

Cara is, and always will be, worth every risk.

GABE'S EPILOGUE

Gabe's epilogue
Present Day...

I still can't believe the shit that just went down with my ex. Hours later, out with my buddies playing poker, and I'm reeling a little bit in shock. But I'm damn grateful too that it's all over, even in spite of that awful ending.

I shudder involuntarily at the memory of the way my ex stormed out of my home a few weeks ago, the horrible things she said. No — *shouted*. For my whole building to hear.

Then, as Drew asks if I'm all in on this hand, I shake off the memory. Screw exes. "I'm definitely in," I say, then slide another chip into the pile on the table at The Happiest Hours, a bar in Venice —

home of my so-called Free At Last party the guys are throwing me.

While we toast to moving on, I vow to focus on my one true love — football. This is my last year in the NFL and I don't need anything keeping me company but the game.

I clink glasses with the guys, and as Drew shuffles the deck to deal the next round, my gaze strays to the window where a sexy-as-sin brunette chats on the phone as she walks a little dog down the street.

The woman's got a swing in her hips and a pouty fullness to her lips. She looks like a piece of candy, all effortlessly delicious in tight jean shorts, cut off and raggedy sexy, and a purple halter top that shows off her pierced belly. I'd like to peel that top off her, lick a path between her tits and down her stomach, then tug on her belly ring with my teeth.

Even though I totally shouldn't be thinking about that.

As I stare unabashedly a little longer, she starts to look damn familiar.

She reminds me vaguely of picnics, barbecues, Thanksgivings. Then, a Christmas party. A moment under the mistletoe, maybe.

Wait.

Hold the hell on.

Is that…?

No fucking way.

Another memory flashes before me of Ellie Snow. One of the times I babysat her.

* * *

Find out what Gabe and Ellie are up to now when they meet again in the dirty, sexy, age-gap (she's 26, he's 36!), fake-dating romance available in KU for FREE in The Good Guy Challenge!

Want a totally free novella? Sign up for my newsletter to receive Most Irresistible Guy, a fun football novella that's only available to subscribers!

USA Today Bestselling contemporary romance!

BEST LAID PLANS, a sexy friends-to-lovers USA Today Bestselling romance!

The Heartbreakers! The USA Today and WSJ Bestselling rock star series of standalone!

P.S. IT'S ALWAYS BEEN YOU, a sweeping, second chance romance!

MY ONE WEEK HUSBAND, a sexy standalone romance!

CONTACT

I love hearing from readers! You can find me on Twitter at LaurenBlakely3, Instagram at LaurenBlakelyBooks, Facebook at LaurenBlakelyBooks, or online at LaurenBlakely.com. You can also email me at laurenblakelybooks@gmail.com

Printed in Great Britain
by Amazon

25151908R00169